DEATH OF
A
HUSSY

D0755658

The Hamish Macbeth series

DEATH OF
A
HUSSY

A Hamish Macbeth Murder Mystery

M. C. Beaton

CONSTABLE • LONDON

CONSTABLE

First published in the USA by St Martin's Press, 1988

First published in the UK by Robinson,
an imprint of Constable & Robinson Ltd., 2008

This edition published by C&R Crime,
an imprint of Constable & Robinson Ltd., 2013

Reprinted in 2017 by Constable

3 5 7 9 10 8 6 4 2

Copyright © M. C. Beaton, 1988

The moral right of the author has been asserted.

*All characters and events in this publication, other than those
clearly in the public domain, are fictitious and any resemblance
to real persons, living or dead, is purely coincidental.*

All rights reserved.
No part of this publication may be reproduced, stored in a retrieval system,
or transmitted, in any form, or by any means, without the prior permission in
writing of the publisher, nor be otherwise circulated in any form of binding or
cover other than that in which it is published and without a similar condition
including this condition being imposed on the subsequent purchaser.

A CIP catalogue record for this book
is available from the British Library.

ISBN 978-1-4721-0524-0

Printed and bound in Great Britain by
CPI Group (UK) Ltd, Croydon CR0 4YY

Papers used by Constable are from well-managed forests
and other responsible sources.

Constable
is an imprint of
Little, Brown Book Group
Carmelite House
50 Victoria Embankment
London EC4Y 0DZ

An Hachette UK Company
www.hachette.co.uk

www.littlebrown.co.uk

The author wishes to thank Hugh Johnston, owner and manager of Golspie Motors Ltd., of Golspie, Sutherland, his service manager, John Mackay, and his mechanic, Bill Brown, for their expert advice, and dedicates this book with gratitude to these three excellent and patient gentlemen of the Scottish Highlands.

Chapter One

In the Highlands in the country places
Where the old plain men have rosy faces,
And the young fair maidens
Quiet eyes.
                                    – R.L. Stevenson

'You might have *known* people really do dress up for dinner in the Highlands.' Maggie Baird shifted her large bulk irritably in the driving seat and crashed the gears horribly.

Beside her in the passenger seat of the battered Renault 5, her niece, Alison Kerr, sat in miserable silence. Her Aunt Maggie had already gone on and on and *on* about Alison's shabby appearance before they left the house. Alison had tried to protest that, had she been warned about this dinner invitation to Tommel Castle, she would have washed and set her hair and possibly bought a new dress. As it was, her black hair was lank and greasy and she wore a plain navy skirt and a white blouse.

As Maggie Baird mangled the car on its way to Tommel Castle – that is, she seemed to

1

wrench the gears a lot and stamp down on the footbrake for no apparent reason at all – Alison sat and brooded on her bad luck.

Life had seemed to take on new hope and meaning when her mother's sister, Maggie Baird, had descended on the hospital where Alison was recovering from lung cancer in Bristol. Alison's parents were both dead. She had, when they were alive, heard little about this Mrs Maggie Baird, except, 'We don't talk about her, dear, and want to have nothing to do with her.'

When she had thought she was about to die, Alison had written to Maggie. After all, Maggie appeared to be her only surviving relative and there should be at least one person to arrange the funeral. Maggie had swept into the patient's lounge, exuding a strong air of maternal warmth. Alison would come with her to her new home in the Highlands and convalesce.

And so Alison had been borne off to Maggie's large sprawling bungalow home on the hills overlooking the sea outside the village of Lochdubh in Sutherland in the very north of Scotland.

The first week had been pleasant. The bungalow was overcarpeted, overwarm, and overfurnished. But there was an efficient housekeeper – what in the old days would have been called a maid of all work – who came up from the village every day to clean and cook. This treasure was called Mrs Todd and although Alison was thirty-one, Mrs Todd treated her like a little girl and made her special cakes for afternoon tea.

By the second week Alison longed to escape from the house. Maggie herself went down to the village to do the shopping but she would never take Alison. Eventually all that maternal warmth faded, to be replaced by a carping bitchiness. Alison, still feeling weak and dazed and gutless after her recent escape from death, could not stand up to her aunt and endured the increasing insults in a morose silence.

Then had come the invitation to dinner from the Halburton-Smythes, local landowners, who lived out on the far side of the village at Tommel Castle, and Maggie had not told her about their going until the very last minute, hence the lank hair and the blouse and skirt.

Maggie crashed the gears again as they went up a steep hill. Alison winced. What a way to treat a car! If she herself could only drive! Oh, to be able to go racing up and over the mountains and to be free and not immured in the centrally heated prison that was Maggie's bungalow. Of course, Alison should just leave and get a job somewhere, but the doctors had told her to take it easy for at least six months and somehow she felt too drained of energy to even try to escape from Maggie. She was terrified of a recurrence of cancer. It was all very well for other people to point out that these days cancer need not be a terminal illness. Alison had had a small part of her lung

3

removed. She was terribly aware of it, imagining a great hole lurking inside her chest. She longed daily for a cigarette and often refused to believe that a diet of forty cigarettes a day had contributed to her illness.

Maggie swung the little red car between two imposing gate posts and up a well-kept drive.

Alison braced herself. What would these people be like?

Priscilla Halburton-Smythe pushed the food around her plate and wished the evening would end. She did not like Maggie Baird, who, resplendent in a huge green and gold caftan, was eating with relish. Her voice was 'county' as she talked to Colonel Halburton-Smythe about the iniquities of poachers, and only Alison knew that Maggie had a talent for sounding knowledgeable on all sorts of subjects she knew little about.

I can't quite make her out, thought Priscilla. She's a great fat woman and quite nasty to that little niece of hers and yet Daddy is going on like an Edwardian gallant. He seems quite taken with her.

She looked again at Alison. Alison Kerr was a thin girl – well, possibly in her thirties, but such a waif that it was hard to think of her as a woman. She had thick horn-rimmed glasses, and her black hair fell in two wings shielding most of her face. She had very good skin, very pale, almost translucent. Priscilla flashed a

4

smile at Alison who scowled and looked at her plate.

Priscilla was everything Alison despised. She was beautiful in a cool poised way with shining pale gold hair worn in a simple style. Her scarlet silk dress with the ruffled Spanish sleeves must have cost a fortune. Her voice was charming and amused.

I would be charming and amused if I lived in a castle and had doting parents, thought Alison bitterly. I know what that smile meant. She's sorry for me. Damn her.

'You will find you have to do a lot of driving in the Highlands, Mrs Baird,' the colonel said.

Maggie sighed and then looked at him with a wicked twinkle in her eyes. 'How true,' she said, 'I'm up and down that road to the village like a tart's drawers.'

There was a little silence. Mrs Halburton-Smythe opened her mouth a little and then shut it again. Then the colonel gave an indulgent laugh. 'It's not London,' he said. 'There isn't an Asian grocer at the corner of every field. You have to make lists, you know. It's quite possible to buy all the groceries for a week in one go. Doesn't that housekeeper of yours do the shopping?'

'I prefer to do it myself,' said Maggie, once more falling into the role of country gentlewoman. 'I like to get the best of everything although Lochdubh is pretty limited. I think the inhabitants must live on a diet of fish fingers.'

'You should take a trip into Inverness and stock up,' said Mrs Halburton-Smythe. 'They've got everything there now. Quite a boom town and expanding every day. Why, I remember not so long ago when it was a sleepy place and they drove the Highland cattle to market through the main street. Now it's all cars, cars, cars.'

'And crime on the increase,' said the colonel. 'What those fools in Strathbane think they're about to leave us without a policeman, I don't know.'

'Hamish!' said Priscilla. 'You didn't tell me.' She smiled at Alison. 'I only arrived last night and haven't caught up with the local news. Hamish gone? Where?'

'They've closed down the police station and taken that lazy lout off to Strathbane,' said her father. 'It's funny, I never thought Macbeth actually did anything. Now he's gone and someone has been netting salmon in the river. At least Macbeth would have found a way to stop it, although he never arrested anyone.'

'But this is dreadful,' exclaimed Priscilla. 'Hamish is a terrible loss to the village.'

'Well, *you* would naturally think so,' said her father acidly.

Priscilla's cool manner seemed ruffled. Oho! thought Alison, I wonder if the daughter of the castle is in love with the absent local copper.

Maggie looked amused. 'If you want to get him back,' she said, 'all you need to do is manufacture some crime in the village.'

She flashed a flirtatious look at the colonel. Priscilla thought, It's as if there's a beauty encased under that layer of fat.

But she said aloud, 'What a good idea. Why don't we organize a meeting in the village hall and put it to the locals.'

The colonel seemed about to protest but the suggestion caught Maggie's imagination. She liked to imagine herself a leader of Highland village society.

'I'll arrange it for you if you like,' she said. 'Alison can help. Or try to help. She's not really good at anything, you know. When shall we have the meeting?'

'Why not this Saturday?' asked Priscilla.

'You are not suggesting you are going to encourage the villagers to commit crimes so as to get Hamish back!' said Mrs Halburton-Smythe.

'Something must be done,' said Priscilla. 'We'll put it to the locals and then take a vote.'

'A vote on what?' demanded her father.

'On whatever suggestions are put up,' said Priscilla evasively. 'There's no need for you to get involved, Daddy. I am sure Mrs Baird and I can handle everything.'

Alison found herself beginning to speculate on this local bobby. He must be someone very special to attract the cool Priscilla. Her mind wandered off into fantasy. What if she helped to get him back, managed to do more than Priscilla? This Hamish Macbeth would be tall and fair and handsome like those paintings of

Bonnie Prince Charlie on the old biscuit tins. He would fall in love with her, Alison, and take her away from Maggie and leave Priscilla with the knowledge that Alison's inner attractions were more important to a man than stereotyped outward beauty. She lacks character in her face, thought Alison, looking under her lashes at Priscilla and trying to find fault.

At last the evening was over. Maggie was wrapped by the butler in a voluminous mink coat. I hope Macbeth isn't into Animal Liberation, thought Alison maliciously. That coat must have taken a whole ranch of minks.

As she was leaving, the colonel suddenly leaned forward and kissed Maggie on the cheek. She flashed him a roguish look and he puffed out his chest and strutted like a bantam.

Oh, dear, thought Priscilla, I wish he wouldn't make such a fool of himself.

She did not know that her father's misplaced gallantry was to start a chain of events which would lead to murder.

Maggie was in a good mood as she drove home through the wintry landscape and under the bright and burning stars of Sutherland. So she could still attract a man. And if she could attract a man when she was like this – well, plump – think what effect she could have if she took herself in hand.

8

It was all the fault of that damned waiter, thought Maggie. Maggie Baird had earned a considerable amount of money during her career. Although she had managed to stay off the streets and had been married and divorced twice, she had made a business out of being mistress to a long string of wealthy men, occasionally straying to the poorer ones for her own amusement. Like most women addicted to food, she also had a tremendous appetite for sex. Unlike most of her sisters on the game, she had squirrelled away her earnings, buying and selling property and investing cleverly. That was when the blow had fallen. Finding herself a very wealthy woman and looking for amusement, Maggie had taken up with a Greek waiter whose swarthy good looks had appealed to her. But for the first time in her life, she had fallen helplessly in love and when she had found that he was taking her money to save enough to marry a young blonde from Stepney, she felt her life was over.

She had bought the bungalow in the Highlands, a place to lick her wounds. She had let the bleach grow out of her hair so that it became its natural brown streaked with grey. She had put on pounds and pounds in weight. She wore tweeds and suede hats and oilskin coats and brogues and everything she could to adopt the character of a Scottish gentlewoman, as if hiding her hurt under layers of fat and country dress.

Taking Alison out of the hospital made her feel good for a while, until the novelty had worn off. Now the pain of the waiter's rejection was fading as well.

'There's life in the old girl yet,' she said cheerfully.

'You mean the car?' asked Alison.

'Me, you fool, not this heap of junk.'

'It's a very nice little car,' said Alison timidly. 'Auntie –'

'I told you not to call me that,' snapped Maggie.

'Sorry ... Maggie. Look, do you think I could take driving lessons? I could do the shopping for you.'

'I've got more to do with my money than pay for your driving lessons,' said Maggie. 'That colonel's quite a lad. His wife looks a bit of a faded nonentity. And that daughter of his! No character.'

'Exactly,' agreed Alison eagerly. Both women fell to trashing Priscilla and arrived home quite pleased with each other for the first time in weeks.

The Highlands of Scotland contain many pretty towns and villages but Strathbane was not one of them. It had been attractive once, but had become a centre for light industry in the early fifties and that had brought people flooding in from the cities. Ugly housing complexes had been thrown up all round; garish supermarkets, discos, and wine bars and all the doubtful benefits of a booming economy had come to Strathbane along with crime and drugs.

Police Constable Hamish Macbeth sadly left the kennels where his dog, Towser, was housed. It was his evening off. He was bored and lonely and he hated Strathbane and he hated Detective Chief Inspector Blair with a passion for moving him out of Lochdubh.

He was sick and tired of the youth of Strathbane with their white pinched faces, their drunkenness, and their obscenities. He was tired of raiding discos for drugs, and bars for drunks, and football matches for hooligans.

He walked along the dirty streets. A thin drizzle was falling. Even the seagulls wheeling under the harsh orange light of the sodium street lamps looked dirty. He leaned on the wall and stared down on the beach. The tide was up; oil glittered on the water and an old sofa with burst springs was slowly being gathered in by the rising tide.

A man reeled past him, then leaned against the sea wall and vomited on to the beach. Hamish shuddered and moved away. He wondered how much longer he could endure this existence. His home in Lochdubh had been the police station, so he did not even have a house to go back to. The neighbours were looking after his hens and his sheep, but he could not expect them to do so indefinitely. Some real estate agent would probably sell the police

11

station. He had left most of his possessions there, refusing to believe his life in Lochdubh was over.

Then there was Mary Graham. PC Graham was Hamish's usual partner on the beat in Strathbane. She was a thin, spare woman with a hard face and dyed blonde hair and a thirst for making as many arrests as possible. She was from the south of Scotland and considered Hamish some sort of half-witted peasant.

Hamish's mind went back and forth and round and round the problem, seeking escape. He could always go back to Lochdubh and take lodgings with someone. He could move his hen houses on to the bit of croft land assigned to him. But, like all crofters, he knew it was impossible to live on small farming alone, trying to wrest a living out of a few stony fields. He could work on the fishing boats, of course.

What hurt most of all was that the people of Lochdubh appeared to have taken his banishment without comment. He felt very friendless.

On Saturday night, the village hall in Lochdubh was crammed to capacity. On the platform facing the audience was the committee made up of Maggie, Alison, Priscilla, and the minister, Mr Wellington, and his large, tweedy wife – who for the first time in her life was outdone in largeness and tweediness.

Maggie Baird was encased in new tweeds and had a suede hat with a pheasant's feather on it on her head. Alison had washed and set her hair for the occasion, perhaps in the hope that the handsome policeman would walk in the door while the meeting was on.

Maggie Baird, much to the annoyance of Mrs Wellington, rose to speak.

'Our local policeman has been sent away because of a lack of crime in the area. I suggest we organize enough crime to make it necessary to send him back.'

There was a roar of approval. Shocked, Mrs Wellington struggled to her feet and held up her hands for silence.

'That is a most dreadful and, if you will forgive me, Mrs Baird, *immoral* suggestion.'

'What would you suggest?' asked Maggie with dangerous sweetness.

'Well, I think we should get up a petition.'

'We'll put it to a vote,' said Maggie. 'All in favour of organizing some crime, raise their hands.'

A forest of hands went up.

'All in favour of a petition?'

Only a few hands went up.

Mr Wellington took the floor. 'You cannot, Mrs Baird, expect us all to break the law.'

'No one said anything about breaking the law,' replied Maggie cheerfully. 'We make it look as if we've got a crime and insist on having the police in. I am going to pass round sheets of paper and you will all write down

13

suggestions. I will report that something of mine, something valuable, has been stolen, and then after a bit I'll say, "Sorry to have wasted your time, it has been found." That sort of thing.'

There was a silence in the hall. Maggie realized furiously that everyone was obviously waiting for Priscilla to say something.

Feudal lot of peasants, thought Maggie angrily.

Priscilla got to her feet. She was wearing a smart grey tailored pin-striped suit with a white blouse, sheer stockings, and patent leather high heels. 'Yes, I think a bit of organized crime is the sensible answer,' said Priscilla. 'My father is having trouble again with poachers. I shall start off with that complaint.'

There was a cheer and a man shouted, 'Good for you. We knew you would think of something.'

In that moment, Alison felt quite warm toward her aunt. It did seem unfair that Maggie should have thought up the scheme only to have everyone give Priscilla all the credit.

Papers were passed around, a few half bottles of whisky were produced, the villagers scribbled busily. The air was soon heavy with the raw smell of alcohol and a fog of cigarette smoke.

When the meeting was over, everyone was

happy with the results – with the exception of Mr and Mrs Wellington, Maggie, and Alison.

'Why did I bother?' fumed Maggie on the road home. 'Did you see that Halburton-Smythe bitch calmly taking the credit for everything? Anyway, my crime is the best and so I shall show them.'

Sergeant MacGregor drove angrily over the twisting Highland roads that led from Cnothan to Lochdubh. Some female had lost her diamond earrings and what should have been handled by that Macbeth fellow was now having to be handled by him, MacGregor.

What made it worse was that this female, this Mrs Baird, had phoned the high-ups in Strathbane and accused them of deliberately encouraging crime in Lochdubh by taking away the village policeman and had threatened to write to *The Times*.

He drove through Lochdubh, remarking sourly to himself that it looked as sleepy as ever, and took the coast road to Maggie's bungalow.

The door was opened by a grim-looking housekeeper wearing a blue cotton dress with a white collar. MacGregor's heart sank. Anyone who could afford to employ a Scottish housekeeper these days and get her to wear a sort of uniform must be stinking rich, and stinking rich meant power, and power meant trouble.

Mrs Baird was all he had feared and anticipated. She was a great, fat woman wearing a tweed suit and heavy brogues. Her thick hair was scraped back in an old-fashioned bun and she had the glacial accents of the upper class. With her on the chintz-covered sofa sat a dab of a woman, peering at him through thick-lensed glasses, whom Mrs Baird introduced as 'my niece, Miss Kerr.'

'You took your time about getting here,' said Maggie.

'Well, I have to come from Cnothan, which is a good wee bit away,' said MacGregor with what he hoped was a placating smile.

'Stop grinning like a monkey and get your notebook out,' ordered Maggie. The housekeeper brought in a tray with a coffee pot, cream, sugar, and only two cups. MacGregor was obviously not going to be offered any.

'When did you first notice the earrings were missing?' asked MacGregor.

'Last night. I've searched the house. Mrs Todd, the housekeeper, is a local woman and above suspicion. But two suspicious-looking hikers were seen hanging about yesterday. They could have got in somehow and taken them.'

'Description?' asked MacGregor, licking his pencil.

'Man and a girl, early twenties. The man had a straggly beard and the girl looked like one of those dreary intellectual types, rather like Miss Kerr here.' Maggie laughed and

Alison winced. 'The man was wearing a camouflage jacket and jeans, and the girl, a red anorak and brown slacks. The man had on a ski cap and the girl was hatless. Her hair was mousy brown.'

MacGregor eventually drove off in a more cheerful frame of mind. He had something concrete to go on. He telephoned from his Land Rover to Strathbane and put out an alert for the hikers. That strange creature, Macbeth, who had had the temerity to solve a murder case in his, MacGregor's, absence, would soon find out his presence was not missed in Lochdubh.

He had only just reached home when a call came through from the chief constable. Colonel Halburton-Smythe demanded the presence of a policeman immediately. Poachers were netting salmon on his river. With a groan, MacGregor set out for Lochdubh again. The colonel insisted on taking the sergeant on a long walk across country to the river and haranguing him on the ineptitude of the police. MacGregor was tired and weary by the time he got back to Cnothan.

But fury gave him energy, fury generated by a call from Strathbane to say that Mrs Baird had telephoned. She had found her lost earrings down the back of the sofa and what was MacGregor doing wasting the force's time by having them look for villainous hikers who did not exist?

Then a phone call came from the Lochdubh

17

Hotel to say that a group of young people were creating a riot in the public bar. MacGregor appealed for back-up and took the road back to Lochdubh to find the public bar empty apart from a few shattered glasses and the owner of the hotel, who was unable to give a clear description of the young people.

By the time he finally got home to bed, he was nearly in tears of rage. Morning found him in a calmer frame of mind. Lochdubh would sink back into its usual peace and quiet.

And then the phone started to ring. A crofter in Lochdubh complained that five of his sheep had been stolen during the night, and a farmer reported that two of his prize cows were missing. The schoolteacher, Miss Monson, called to say that drugs had been found in a classroom.

Again MacGregor telephoned for help, only to be asked wearily why he couldn't handle things himself – that is, until he got to the tale of the drugs in the classroom. Detective Chief Inspector Blair and a team of detectives and forensic men were despatched from Strathbane only to find that the drugs in the classroom were packets of baking soda. 'Silly me,' said the giggling schoolteacher, and Blair took his anger out on MacGregor, who had no one to take it out on except his wife, and he was afraid of her.

The amazing thing about British policewomen is that a surprising proportion of them are attractive. And so PC Hamish Macbeth could not help wondering why he had the ill luck to be saddled with such a creature as Mary Graham on his beat. PC Graham, he reflected, looked like one of those women you see in German war films. Not only was there the dyed blonde hair, but she had staring ice-blue eyes, a mouth like a trap, and an impeccable uniform with a short tailored skirt which showed strong muscular legs encased in black tights – not fine sheer tights worn by some of the younger policewomen, but thick wool ones, and her shoes were like black polished glass.

It was a sunny day as they walked side by side along the waterfront, past closed bars smelling of last night's drunks; past shuttered warehouses falling into ruin, relics of the days when Strathbane was a small busy port; past blocks of houses thrown up in the fifties during that period when all architects seem to have sold their souls to Stalin, and had erected towers of concrete very like their counterparts in Moscow. The balconies had once been painted jolly primary colours, but now long trails of rust ran down the cracked concrete of the buildings in which elevators had long since died, and rubbish lay in heaps on the sour earth of what was originally intended to be a communal garden.

'I always keep ma eyes and ears open,' Mary was saying. She had a whining singsong voice. 'I hae noticed, Macbeth, you're apt to turn a blind eye tae too many things.'

'Such as?' asked Hamish while in his mind he picked her up and threw her over the sea wall and then watched her sink slowly beneath the oily surface of the rising tide.

'Two days ago there were these two drunks fighting outside The Glen bar. All you did was separate them and send them off home. I wanted to arrest them and would hae done had I not seen that wee boy acting suspiciously over at the supermarket.'

Hamish sighed. There was no point replying. Mary saw villains everywhere. But her next words nearly roused him to a fury, and it took a great deal to rouse Hamish Macbeth. 'I felt it was ma duty to put in a report about you,' she said. 'It is cramping my style to have to walk the beat wi' a Highland layabout. The trouble wi' you Highlanders is you just want to lie on your backs all day long. You know whit they say, *mañana* is too *urgent* a word for you.' Mary laughed merrily at her own wit. 'So I said I would never rise in the force, having to patrol wi' a deadbeat like you, and asked for a change.'

'That would be nice,' said Hamish.

Mary threw him a startled look. 'I'm surprised you're taking it so well.'

'Of course I am taking it well. Ye dinnae think I enjoy walking along on a fine day wi' a sour-faced bitch like you,' said Hamish in a light pleasant voice, although Priscilla, for example, would have recognized, by the sudden sibilancy of it, that Hamish was furious.

'Wass I not saying chust the other day,' said Hamish dreamily, 'that it was sore luck getting landed wi' you instead of someone like Pat Macleod.' Pat Macleod was a curvaceous brunette of a policewoman who wore sheer stockings instead of tights. Every policeman who had seen her flashing her thighs in the canteen as she deliberately hitched up her short skirt to sit down could bear witness to that.

Mary could hardly believe her ears. She would never for a moment have dreamt that PC Macbeth would even think of insulting her. She did not know that her contempt for him was largely based on jealousy. Macbeth, in a short time, had made himself popular on the beat and householders preferred to bring their troubles to him rather than to Mary.

'I have never been so insulted in all my life,' she said.

'Oh, come now, wi' a face and manner like yours, you must have been,' said Hamish who, like all normally polite and kind people, was relishing the rarity of being truly and thoroughly rude.

'You're jist mad because Blair winkled ye oot o' your cosy number in Lochdubh,' sneered Mary. 'And you claim to have solved them murders! You! You're no' a man. I could beat the living daylights oot o' you any day.'

'Try it,' said Hamish.

She squared up to him. 'I warn ye. I'm a black belt in karate.'

'Behave yourself, woman,' said Hamish, suddenly sick to death of her.

With amazing speed, he moved in under her guard, swept her up in his lanky arms, dumped her head first in an enormous plastic rubbish bin, and, deaf to her cries, strolled off.

That's that, he thought with gloomy satisfaction, I may as well go back to the police station and resign.

The desk sergeant looked up as Hamish ambled in. 'Upstairs, Macbeth. The super's screaming for you.'

'So soon?' said Hamish, surprised. 'Did PC Graham fly in on her broomstick? Never mind. Better get it over with.'

'Come in, come in, Hamish,' said Superintendent Peter Daviot. 'Sit down, man. Tea?'

'Yes, thank you,' said Hamish, sitting down on a chair facing the desk and putting his peaked cap on his knees.

'It seems, Hamish, that there's been a bit of a crime wave in Lochdubh and Sergeant MacGregor's being run ragged.'

'Is he now?' asked Hamish with a smile. He did not like MacGregor.

'Milk and sugar? Right. Here you are. Yes, on due consideration, we have decided you should finish up the week here and return to Lochdubh. Here are the keys to the station.'

'Thank you.' Hamish felt suddenly bleak. Why had he risen to that stupid Graham woman's insults?

The door opened and Detective Chief

Inspector Blair heaved his large bulk into the room. 'Oh, you're here, are you?' he said nastily when he saw Hamish.

'Yes,' said Mr Daviot. 'It seems you made a bad mistake in suggesting that Hamish be taken away from Lochdubh. There's been nothing but crime for the past few days.'

'I know,' said Blair heavily. 'I've been there on a drugs report. Baking soda, it turned oot tae be.' His Glasgow accent grew stronger in his irritation. 'Dae ye know what I think? I think them damp villagers are making up crimes so as tae get this pillock back.'

The superintendent's face froze. 'Mind your language in front of me, Mr Blair,' he said. 'Are you questioning the word of Colonel Halburton-Smythe, for example?'

'No, no,' said Blair hurriedly. 'But it did look a bit suspicious, ye ken, considering nothing happens there from the one year's end tae the other.'

'Except murder,' put in Hamish.

'Do not forget Hamish solved that woman's murder,' said the superintendent. 'I am just telling him he must go back and take up his duties there.'

'Uh-uh!' said Blair, his face creased into an unlovely smile. 'Why I came up, Mr Daviot, is to tell you we might be discussing Macbeth's dismissal from the force.'

'What! Why?'

'He assaulted PC Graham.'

'You assaulted a policewoman, Hamish?'

'It was self-defence, sir.'

'Haw! Haw! Haw!' roared Blair.

'Will you stop cackling, Blair, and give me an outline of the complaint?'

'PC Graham has just come into the station. She said she was patrolling the beat when Macbeth here suddenly picked her up and threw her in a rubbish bin.'

'Is this true, Macbeth?' No more 'Hamish.'

'She said she could beat me up and approached me in a threatening manner,' said Hamish. 'I was fed up wi' her. I chust picked up the lassie and dumped her in wi' the rubbish.'

'I can hardly . . . this is very serious . . . very serious indeed. Oh, what is it, Sergeant?'

The desk sergeant had just entered. 'It's three women and a man frae the tower blocks,' he said. 'They say they've come to defend Macbeth here. They say they saw Graham attacking him and Macbeth being forced to defend himself. They say when they helped Graham out of the bin, she said she was going to get Macbeth charged with assault and they say if that's the case they will all go to court as witnesses for Macbeth's defence.'

'We must not let this get into the newspapers,' said the superintendent, horrified. 'Get rid of these people, Sergeant, and say that Macbeth is not being charged. Shut Graham up at all costs. Good heavens, just think what the tabloids could make of this. Macbeth, I suggest you go back to your quarters and pack and leave for Lochdubh in the morning. Blair, I am surprised at you! In a situation as potentially explosive and damaging to the police as this you should get your facts right. Macbeth, wipe that smile off your face and get going!'

Chapter Two

And with the morn those angel faces smile,
Which I have loved long since, and lost awhile.
　　　　　　　 – Cardinal John Henry Newman

At a new roundabout on the outskirts of Strath-bane stood Hamish Macbeth, a suitcase in one hand. In the other, he held a rope as a leash for Towser, whose own had mysteriously disappeared in the kennels. Towser, a yellowish mongrel, was subdued. He had been kennelled with police dogs, large nasty-looking German shepherds, and had lived for a short time in a state of terror.

There was no reason for Hamish to be standing in a fine drizzle trying to hitch a lift. A police car would have driven him to Lochdubh in the afternoon, but Hamish felt he could not wait that long.

One car after another slowed at the roundabout and then drove past the solitary figure with the battered suitcase and dog. Many people firmly believed you had to have a death wish to give a lift to a stranger these days.

Hamish looked around. There was a thick stand of bushes behind him. He walked into their shelter, opened his case, took out his policeman's tunic, and after tugging off his old sweater, put it on. He was already wearing his regulation trousers. He also fished out his peaked hat and knocked it back into shape and put it on his head.

'I told you, you shouldn't be driving without a licence,' said Mrs Mary Webb to her husband, Bert, as the tall, thin figure of a policeman stepped out into the road just before the round-about and held up his hand. Bert Webb slowed to a halt, his heart hammering. 'Whatever happens, keep your mouth shut,' he hissed to his wife.

He rolled down the window. 'Good day, Officer,' he said with an ingratiating leer. 'What can we do for you?'

'I was wondering if you were travelling anywhere near the village of Lochdubh,' said Hamish.

'We are going farther north,' said Bert uneasily. 'The nearest we get to Lochdubh is the Ardest crossroads.'

'That would do me just fine,' said Hamish. 'I can walk from there easily.'

A look of relief wiped the worry from Bert's face. 'You mean you want a lift?'

'If you would be so kind.'

Relief made Bert hearty. 'Jump in the back,' he said.

28

'Thank you very much,' said Hamish with a sweet smile. 'I will just be getting my dog.' And he disappeared back into the bushes beside the road where he had left Towser.

'Dog!' exclaimed Mary Webb. 'And us with our new seat covers.' She twisted her head and looked at the back seat which was covered in imitation fur fabric of a leopard skin pattern.

'Shut up!' snapped Bert, uneasy again. 'It may be some sort of trick.'

His wife looked at him in alarm but had no time to say anything, for the back door of the car opened and PC Macbeth and a wet Towser climbed inside, Hamish pulling his suitcase in after him.

Hamish tried to make conversation but found it very hard going. Mary Webb was thinking furiously, Perhaps it isn't Bert's licence, perhaps it's those library books I never took back. Then there was that restaurant. They forgot to charge Bert for the drinks and he never said a word . . .

Bert was thinking of the young girl with whom he had enjoyed a brief fling down in Worcester three months ago. He was a shop fitter and travelled around the country. The girl had looked awfully young. What if she was under sixteen?

Hamish finally fell silent. His thoughts turned to Lochdubh. He was still saddened by the way in which all his friends had taken his banishment without any fuss. He had phoned the hotel the night before and had told Mr

Johnson, the manager, of his imminent return and Johnson had taken it calmly, almost coolly, in fact.

'Here we are, Officer!' said Bert with forced joviality. 'The Ardest turning.'

Hamish thanked them and climbed out with suitcase and dog. He touched his cap as the Webbs drove off, the Webbs who were now full of indignant rage at having been forced to give a lift to what had turned out to be nothing more sinister than a scrounging copper.

Towser turned slowly in the direction of Lochdubh, rather like an overstuffed armchair turning around on its castors. He sniffed the air and slowly his tail curved over his back.

A shaft of sunlight struck through the grey clouds, a William Blake shaft of sunlight. All it lacked were the angels. The wind was from the west holding an underlying touch of warmth. Above the shaggy heath of Sutherland soared the mountains, rising up to heaven, away and beyond the antlike machinations of the police force.

Hamish took the rope from around Towser's neck and the dog surged forward down the road to Lochdubh, stopping every now and then to look back and make sure his master was following.

Hoisting his suitcase up on to his shoulder, Hamish stepped out smartly and the sky above grew brighter and brighter and the wind in the heather sang a welcome home.

* * *

'Thank goodness the sun is shining,' said Priscilla. 'Are you sure he said he would be here sometime this morning, Mr Johnson?'

'That's what he said,' remarked the hotel manager. 'Said he couldn't wait and he would hitch a lift.'

'Maybe he can't get a lift,' worried Priscilla. 'One of us should have gone and collected him.'

'And spoil the surprise? No, better this way. Dougie, the gamekeeper, is posted up on the hill and he'll wave a flag when he sees him coming.'

Priscilla shook her head doubtfully, having visions of lazy Hamish stretched out asleep in the back seat of some limousine and unable to be spotted by even such an eagle eye as Dougie's. 'Everything's ready anyway,' she said looking around.

In the centre of the village stood a raised platform that was normally used for school prize-giving day. Already seated on it, furtively sipping something out of a silver flask, was Maggie Baird with the shadow that was Alison beside her. Mrs Wellington sat on Maggie's other side with her husband, the minister, and beside them were Priscilla's mother and father.

Over the street hung a banner saying, 'Welcome Home, Hamish,' and the school choir was lined up in front of the platform, ready to burst into song. Beside them stood the small band – one accordionist, one fiddle player, and the schoolteacher, Miss Monson, seated at the battered upright piano which was usually housed in the school hall.

Jessie and Nessie Currie, the village spinsters, were ready with *their* music, 'My Heart and I.' They had never been known to sing anything else.

And then from the hill above the village, Dougie frantically waved his huge St Andrew's flag in the air. Maggie Baird walked to the front of the platform, stood before the microphone, and took a speech out of her capacious handbag while Mrs Wellington obviously bristled with outrage.

The band struck up 'Westering Home' and the little schoolchildren sang the words in their clear Highland voices. Ragged cheering broke out from the far end of the village.

Alison craned her head forwards and looked along the village street.

Her first sight of Hamish Macbeth sent all her rosy fantasies crashing into ruins. He was tall and thin and gangling with fiery red hair showing under his peaked cap. He looked half delighted and half embarrassed, and as he drew near the platform he actually blushed.

Hamish was trying very hard not to cry. He was making all sorts of grateful promises. No more laziness. No more lolling about. He would, in future, be hardworking and never, ever would he give the powers that be any excuse to send him away again.

He looked up at the platform and his eyes sharpened. The band and the choir had fallen silent. A large woman, a stranger to him, was giving him a speech of welcome. He studied her curiously, his eyes taking in the too-new tweeds, the heavy face, and the autocratic manner. He was forcibly reminded of a competent actress playing the part of a gentlewoman.

There was something about her that disturbed him and as she came to the end of her speech, she drooped one eyelid at him in a definite wink. In that moment, he had an odd feeling that inside that fat tweed-covered body was a slim beauty who had put on some sort of middle-aged disguise for a joke.

And then he realized he was being asked to make a speech.

He climbed up on to the platform, his eyes resting briefly on Alison Kerr and then turning to Priscilla, who had joined her parents. His face lit up and he gave Priscilla a singularly sweet smile.

He's not bad, thought Alison, not bad at all. He had, she noticed for the first time, hazel eyes fringed with thick lashes.

'Thank you all,' said Hamish shyly. 'You haff made me most welcome. I don't know quite what to say. Och, just thank you all from the bottom o' my heart.'

Miss Monson began to play and Nessie and Jessie burst into their well-known rendering of 'My Heart And I.' When they had finished,

Priscilla jumped to her feet. 'Three cheers for Hamish,' she shouted. And Hamish blushed as the cheers rang out and felt that awful lump in his throat. He wanted to get away and be by himself, but there was a welcome buffet luncheon laid out in the Lochdubh Hotel and more speeches, and so he forced himself to talk to everyone and try not to feel he did not deserve any of it.

Priscilla came up to him and kissed him lightly on the cheek. 'Stick it out a bit longer, Hamish,' she whispered. 'It'll soon be over and then you can go home.' Hamish looked at her with quick gratitude and then found he was beginning to enjoy himself.

'Well, copper,' said a throaty voice, 'aren't you going to thank me?'

He looked down at Maggie Baird. He gave her a puzzled look and then his eyes began to dance with mischief. 'Are you then the leader of the Lochdubh Mafia?' he asked. 'All thae crimes had poor Sergeant MacGregor not knowing whether he was coming or going.'

Maggie gave a jolly laugh. 'Someone had to think of something,' she said. 'You were very much missed and now I have met you, I can understand why.'

'You are Mrs Baird,' said Hamish. 'You arrived after I left for Strathbane.'

'Yes.' Maggie became aware that Alison was tugging furtively at her sleeve, obviously hoping for an introduction, and she swung her great bulk a little way around so that Alison was shielded from Hamish. 'I don't know if I'll stay long,' went on Maggie airily, 'but this little place amuses me for the moment.'

'If you like peace and quiet, it'll grow on you,' said Hamish amiably. 'I do not think I haff been introduced to this young lady.' He looked over Maggie's shoulder at Alison.

'Oh, this is my niece, Alison Kerr. She's just recovered from cancer which is why she looks a bit ratty.'

Alison winced and Hamish said quickly, 'You look chust fine to me, Miss Kerr. You must still be feeling awfy frightened. I mean, you must keep worrying that it might come back.'

'Yes,' said Alison gratefully. 'It's made me an awful coward, the fear, I mean. I'm frightened of my own shadow.'

'Well, I suppose that's as good an excuse as any,' said Maggie nastily.

'One o' my cousins had an operation for cancer,' Hamish went on as if Maggie hadn't spoken. 'He's fine now. The fear goes away after a bit. It's a bit like getting over the death of someone you loved.'

Maggie gave a musical laugh and her blue eyes looked flirtatiously up into Hamish's own. 'Is this evening going to turn into a therapy session, or are you going to pay some attention to your saviour?'

'Oh, aye,' said Hamish with a grin. 'I'm grateful to you, Mrs Baird.'

Maggie put her hand on his arm. 'And how are you going to show that gratitude, Officer?'

He was suddenly aware of her overpowering sexuality, of the expensive French perfume she wore, of being enclosed between walls of suffocating intimacy, and instinctively drew back. He thought, This is what a woman must feel like when a man is undressing her with his eyes.

He hailed the arrival of Mrs Todd, Maggie's housekeeper, with relief. 'Good evening, Mrs Todd,' he said. 'It's a while since I've seen you.'

Mrs Todd was a small, sturdy woman dressed, despite the cold evening, in a black silk gown embroidered with jet that looked like an Edwardian relic. She ignored Hamish and Maggie and said to Alison, 'Are you all right, Miss Kerr? I hope the festivities aren't too much for you.'

Mrs Todd's normally hard features were softened by a maternal smile. 'Thank you,' said Alison in a little girl voice. 'I'm feeling fine.'

'I've just been up to the house and put a hot water bottle in your bed and a thermos of milk on the table,' said Mrs Todd. 'You're to drink every drop of that milk, mind!'

'Yes, Mrs Todd,' said Alison meekly. Normally she was grateful for the housekeeper's maternal warmth but just at that moment, she wished Mrs Todd would go away, that Maggie would go away, and leave her to talk to this odd policeman who was the first person who had ever guessed how she really felt.

'You wouldn't think I had good central heating,' said Maggie crossly.

'There's nothing mair comforting than a nice hot water bottle,' said Mrs Todd firmly.

Maggie saw Colonel Halburton-Smythe and decided to go flirt with him to liven up the evening and try her hand with the copper later on. Alison watched her go with relief but then found that Mrs Todd was determined to stay. Hamish talked for a little to both Alison and Mrs Todd and then was claimed by Priscilla.

'The guests are thinning out,' said Priscilla. 'Not long to go, Hamish. How's Mrs Todd enjoying her job as housekeeper?'

'She's fond of that niece, Alison,' said Hamish. 'I suppose she enjoys the money. Mrs Baird is supposed to be rich. Also, it gives Mrs Todd an interest. She hasn't done much since her husband died.'

'When was that again?' asked Priscilla.

'Two years? Three? Can't quite remember myself.'

'And what do you make of Mrs Baird?'

Hamish frowned. 'She makes me uneasy,' he said. 'She's the sort of woman who creates violence. I think she's a bad woman.'

'Why, Hamish Macbeth! You old-fashioned thing!'

'No, I didnae mean scarlet woman. She's spiteful to that niece of hers. She likes to be the centre of attention. She likes excitement. She think she likes affairs and yet she's too fat to have much hope at the moment.'

'I wouldn't be too sure of that,' said Priscilla, watching her father's flushed and excited face as he spoke to Maggie Baird.

Maggie was enjoying herself. She was aware, out of the corner of her eye, of Mrs Halburton-Smythe's disapproval and that gave her a feeling of elation. A jealous woman acted on Maggie's spirits like a shot of adrenalin. There was a long mirror beside her on the wall. She turned to look at herself.

Robert Burns wrote:

> O wad some Pow'r the giftie gie us,
> To see oursels as others see us,
> It wad frae mony a blunder free us,
> And foolish notion.

But Maggie Baird saw herself for the first and last time in her life as she really was and instead of freeing her from foolish notions, it set in motion a catastrophic chain of events.

To see oneself as one really is – if one is ever unlucky enough to have that experience – is quite shattering. The veil of illusions and little vanities is rudely ripped aside. Maggie saw clearly a fat tweedy woman with once beautiful eyes narrowed by fat cheeks. She saw all the pettiness and meanness of soul. She saw the iron grey hair. She looked not only her age but a good bit more. Her hand fluttered up to her cheek in a helpless motion and she turned the colour of mud. She gasped for breath and swayed and the colonel shouted with alarm and rushed to support her.

Dr Brodie, the village doctor, came bustling up. 'Pills,' croaked Maggie. 'Handbag.'

The doctor called for a glass of water while he rummaged in Maggie's handbag, stopping for an instant to look in dazed surprise at a packet of condoms before he found the pills.

Maggie gulped down the pills and slowly her colour began to return. 'I'd better phone for the ambulance,' said Dr Brodie.

'No,' said Maggie weakly. 'I had a bit of a shock. I thought I saw someone I knew. I'll be all right. I hate hospitals. Get me home.'

The competent Mrs Todd drove Maggie and Alison home. Maggie went straight to bed, but did not go to sleep. She lay awake a long time. She quickly forgot that insight into her soul and remembered only her physical appearance. She who had once been famous for her beauty had degenerated into a fat frump. And all because of one faithless greasy waiter. She must have been mad. She remembered looking across at Priscilla as the doctor had helped her from the room. Priscilla, tall and blonde and groomed, seemed to Maggie to be everything that she herself had lost.

She struck the bedclothes with her fat fist. 'I'm not finished yet,' she said aloud. 'Look at Joan Collins!'

The little spark that the colonel's kiss had kindled grew into a flame of ambition. She lay awake long into the night, making plans.

Hamish walked slowly along the waterfront with Priscilla in the direction of the police station with Towser plodding along behind. The party was over. He was deeply grateful for his welcome and yet glad he no longer had to endure any of it. He did not like being the focus of attention and shrewdly judged all the celebration of his return would be followed by a backlash, the village wondering why they had gone to such lengths to get diffident and lazy Hamish back again.

He opened the kitchen door to the police station. 'You'd better take a look at your living room,' said Priscilla's voice behind him. He pushed open the door of the living room and blinked at the array of flower arrangements. 'It's like a funeral,' he said, closing the door quickly. 'I'll make us some coffee.'

'It was Mrs Bisset and Mrs Wellington. You know they do the flowers for the church,' said Priscilla, sitting down on a kitchen chair. She took off her coat and eased it on to the back of the chair. 'Who on earth did Maggie Baird see at that party to give her such a shock?'

Hamish shook his head. 'She was looking in the mirror. Whoever it was certainly gave her a bad fright. Where does she come from?'

'London, I believe. We had her and that

niece over for dinner. Odd woman. Quite spiteful to the niece and quite repulsive looking, but Daddy was taken with her. I gather you guessed that the sudden outburst of crime in Lochdubh was to lure you back.'

'I wisnae quite sure,' said Hamish with a slow smile, 'until I saw the welcome I got. I was so low in spirits in Strathbane, I thought you had all forgotten about me.' He put two cups and saucers on the table. 'Still unmarried?' he asked casually.

'Yes, still unmarried. Still training in computers. Going to be a programmer. Think I'll make a good yuppie?'

'You look what everyone believes a female yuppie to look like,' said Hamish.

'With all the yuppie-bashing around, I don't know if that's a compliment or not.'

'It's a compliment. You look awfy pretty – as usual.'

The last was said in a matter-of-fact way. Hamish, thought Priscilla, was no longer shy in her company.

The following morning, before Maggie awoke, Alison went out to the garage and looked longingly at the little red Renault. In the post that morning, she had received a notification that her driving test was to be held in three weeks' time in Lochdubh. When she had first arrived, she had written off for a test, confident that her benevolent aunt would surely allow her to learn to drive. That was when Maggie had been warm and kindly.

To learn to drive had become an obsession with Alison. In her dreams at night, she soared up and down the Highland roads, competent behind the wheel.

She should move to the nearest town, she lectured herself, get a job and get a car on the pay-up. Gutless, she raged at herself. But she was gutless. Her growing dislike of Maggie and her longing for freedom were not strong enough to enable her to face the world on her own.

She pushed her lank hair out of her eyes and crunched across the gravel to the bungalow which every day seemed more like a prison.

It was too warm, too characterless, decorated in interior designer's brown and cream with glass-topped tables; glass dining table and glass coffee table on wrought iron legs and little glass side tables. The air always seemed to smell of window cleaner, for the efficient Mrs Todd was always polishing and shining the glass. Despite the kindness of Mrs Todd, the kitchen was hardly the refuge it should have been. With its looped-back red and white checked gingham curtains, red geraniums in bowls, and glittering white Formica work surfaces, it looked as sterile as a stage set.

Mrs Todd had not yet arrived. Alison made herself a cup of coffee and tried not to want a cigarette. Then she heard Maggie lumbering down the stairs, and her thin shoulders hunched as if to ward off the verbal blows about to descend on her.

To her surprise, Maggie was dressed. Usually she spent the mornings wandering around in a nightdress and dressing gown.

'I'm leaving today,' said Maggie abruptly.

Alison felt a rush of relief. Maggie was abandoning her and so she would need to make a life for herself after all.

'I want you to stay here and look after things,' said Maggie. 'You can type, can't you?'

Alison nodded.

'Well, on the desk in the study you'll find a pile of tapes. I've been dictating my life story. I want you to type it out. High time you earned your keep.'

'If you had let me learn to drive,' said Alison defensively, 'I could have taken a job in the village.'

'What you would have earned in the village would barely have paid for the petrol,' snapped Maggie. 'I'll be away a few months.'

'When are you leaving?' asked Alison.

'Any moment now,' said Maggie, squinting at her wristwatch. 'The man from Chisholm's is coming.'

Ian Chisholm, the local garage owner, had a large antique Daimler which was usually hired only for weddings and funerals. 'I'm getting him to take me down to Inverness,' went on Maggie. 'I'll do some shopping, have dinner, and take the sleeper.'

'What are you going to do?' asked Alison, beginning to brighten. Maggie was obviously not taking her car. She always left the keys in the ignition. Now, if she would only leave those keys behind, then . . .

'I'm going to do a bit of work on myself,' said Maggie. 'I've let myself go to seed. Makes two of us, hey? Although I used to be beautiful and you quite obviously never were.'

All in that moment, Alison reflected that Maggie was indeed very like her sister, Alison's late mother. Alison's mother had been a colourless woman compared to Maggie, but she would say things just as Alison was preparing to go off to a school dance like, 'I've done my best, but you'll never be a beauty, dear.' People always said things about words not hurting you, thought Alison miserably, but they hurt like hell, the insults piling up until one's self-esteem begins slowly to crumble under the sheer weight of them.

She thought of Maggie's mild heart attack, if that's what it had been, the evening before. She thought of Maggie's money. She, Alison, was Maggie's only relative. Had Maggie made a will? What if Maggie should die and leave her the house and the car and the money? Alison half closed her eyes. She would redecorate the house and sweep away the brown and cream and the glass tables and make it a homey place.

'Take that silly look off your face,' said Maggie. 'Oh, here's Mrs Todd. Go off and get started on those tapes, Alison. I want the whole thing typed up by the time I get back.'

Alison rose and went through to the room off the sitting room which Maggie called her study. It had a workmanlike desk, an electric typewriter, and there, sure enough, were the tapes and a recorder. Alison had never seen Maggie at work. Maggie must have dictated the tapes during the nights, Alison thought, or have done them some time in the past before she came north.

She began to listen to the first tape, her eyes slowly widening in horror. It was pornography. But then Maggie's life had obviously been pornographic. The first chapter dealt with Maggie's loss of virginity. Alison did not yet know that it was mild stuff compared to what was to follow.

Then above the sound of Maggie's voice, she heard the Daimler arriving. She switched off the tapes and went outside. Only one small suitcase was being loaded into the car. Mrs Todd was standing respectfully while Maggie rapped out last-minute instructions. 'And take all my clothes from my bedroom and send them to Oxfam or the Salvation Army,' Maggie was saying. 'I leave it to you. And see that Alison gets on with typing out that life story of mine and doesn't moon around getting lazier and spottier.'

Alison, whose clear skin was her one vanity, had found two small spots on her forehead that morning. Trust Maggie to have noticed them!

And then Maggie suddenly threw her arms around Alison and gave her a warm hug. 'Look after yourself, pet,' she said. 'That nasty cancer isn't going to come back. Just take care of yourself.' There were tears in her blue eyes.

Alison hugged her back, startled and then moved.

Maggie climbed into the old Daimler, waved her fat hand once, and the car drove off.

Alison and Mrs Todd returned to the house and sat and talked about nothing in particular and then Alison steeled herself to go back to her typing. The sudden burst of affection she had felt for Maggie after that hug was fast evaporating, to be replaced with the calculating thought, Why, the old bag's fond of me. Will she leave me her money? Please God, she leaves me her money.

Alison was a good typist. She finished the first chapter, part of her mind noting mechanically that the writing was so bad, it would surely never get published, and the other part thinking, Did she leave the car keys, and if she did, what could I do?

At last she could not bear it any longer. She went out to the garage and looked in the window of the Renault. There were the keys. Her heart began to hammer against her ribs. She felt the crumpled piece of paper that was the notification for her driving test. But even if she learned to drive, the insurance might not cover her. Perhaps the insurance covered only Maggie's driving.

She ran back into the house and began to search through the jumble of papers in the desk drawer. There it was. She opened the form up and scanned it. The insurance would cover her.

But who would teach her to drive?

And then she thought of Hamish Macbeth.

Chapter Three

*Experience is the name everyone gives to
their mistakes.*

           – Oscar Wilde

The bell at the front door of the police station
rang.

Hamish sighed and put down the book he
was reading. No one in the village ever rang
the front doorbell. They always came to the
kitchen door. The ring at the front usually
meant some sort of official visit.

He was not in uniform, but it was ten
o'clock at night and he had every reason to be
off duty. He paused for a moment, wondering
whether to answer it. Memories of Strathbane
were still sharp in his mind. What if that
dreadful policewoman had decided to press
charges for assault?

The bell went again. He had a superstitious
feeling he should not answer it. The wind
howled outside. Giving himself a shake, he
went slowly to the front of the police station
and opened the door.

Alison Kerr stood there, blinking up at him owlishly in the blue light from the police lamp over the door.

'Come in,' said Hamish. 'It's a dreadful night. What's happened?'

'Nothing,' said Alison as he closed the door behind her. 'I just wanted to ask you a favour.'

'Then come through to the kitchen and I'll make us a cup of tea. My! You're soaked through. Give me your coat.'

He helped Alison out of her wet raincoat and then ushered her into the long narrow kitchen at the back of the house.

Alison sat down at the table and took off her glasses and wiped the raindrops from them with the edge of her skirt. The kitchen was warm and cheerful and Hamish, in a checked shirt and corduroys, reassuringly nonofficial.

'Now,' said Hamish, 'what's all this about?'

Alison clutched the mug of tea in both hands. 'Maggie's gone,' she said. 'She says she will be away a few months and . . .' – Alison braced herself for the lie to come – 'she says she doesn't mind if I learn to drive and my test is in three weeks' time and there isn't an instructor in Lochdubh and I don't know anyone and I wondered if you would . . . could . . . possibly . . . and . . .'

She fell silent and a large tear rolled down her nose and plopped on the table.

'You want me to teach you how to drive,' said Hamish amiably. 'Och, I see no reason why not. You do have a provisional licence, do you not?'

'Yes,' said Alison shakily. 'I've had it quite a long time. You see, Mr Macbeth, I've always wanted to drive and ... and ... Maggie said she wouldn't let me touch the car but she relented just before she left.'

'Where has she gone?' asked Hamish while all the time he was thinking, Mrs Baird never gave this wee lassie permission to use the car. She's lying. But then I am not supposed to know that.

'She's gone to have herself done up,' said Alison, and then blushed furiously. 'I mean, she's going to become beautiful again, she says.'

'There must be a gentleman in the picture.'

'No ... no ... I don't think so. I think she just decided to take herself in hand. But about the driving. When can we start? I've only got three weeks.'

'Well, things here are awfy quiet unless someone starts inventing crimes again. What about coming around here at six tomorrow evening?'

'But it's such a long way and I can't drive,' bleated Alison.

'Oh, I forgot. I'll drive out then – at six.'

'Thank you,' said Alison 'I'm sorry I'm so emotional about it all. But you see, it's my first step towards independence. I mean, I used to be awfully confident and brave before I got cancer.'

And in that heady moment, Alison believed what she had just said, forgetting the years of rabbitlike scurrying to work as secretary to the boss of a small firm which manufactured electrical components. She had been bored out of her skull but had never had the courage to hand in her notice. The factory had been on a failing industrial estate on the outskirts of Bristol, a wasteland of crumbling buildings and old beds, tyres, armchairs, and cookers, as the townspeople used it as a dump.

Hamish watched her sympathetically, reflecting that Maggie was probably the present villain in Alison's life. Timid people always had to have a villain around to maintain some shreds of self-respect. They always thought, If he or she, the husband or mother, or whoever, weren't around, then we would become successful and bold and glamorous, and when the bullies were removed from the scene by divorce or death, the rabbits immediately set out on their quests to find replacements.

'It's so beautiful up here,' Alison was saying. 'I feel in my bones that I am really a Highlander.'

'It's quiet for a lady like yourself used to town life,' commented Hamish, pouring more tea.

'Oh, things always happen to me,' said Alison airily. 'Adventure seems to follow me around.'

The wind tore at the house and Hamish repressed a shudder. He was already regretting his generous impulse to give Alison driving lessons. He was uneasy about the whole thing, and it was not because he knew Alison was lying.

'What's the driving test like?' asked Alison.

'Well, it's not so bad here as in the towns,' said Hamish. 'There are no roundabouts or traffic lights. But they're very strict for all that. I don't want to depress you, but the failure rate in the British driving test is fifty-three per cent. You have to train your mind to pass as well as concentrating on your driving ability. Stop worrying too much about the test and work instead at becoming a skilled driver. At the test, before you even get in the car; before you can even slide behind the wheel, you must be able to read a car number plate at a distance of sixty seven feet. So make sure your glasses are up to the mark. Then after your test, you will be given an oral exam on the Highway Code. Have you got a copy?'

'Oh, yes,' said Alison. She sighed. 'I wish I were more experienced.' She cast a sudden flirtatious look at Hamish and blushed and blew her nose on a rather grubby handkerchief to cover her confusion.

'I'd better be running you back,' said Hamish.

'That's very kind of you.' Alison got to her feet and gazed up adoringly into Hamish's hazel eyes, but the policeman's eyes were a polite blank and he seemed to have retreated to somewhere inside of himself. Alison felt exactly as if she had made a bold pass and been ruthlessly snubbed.

It's all the fault of that Priscilla, thought Alison, she doesn't want him for herself and yet she won't let him go. By the time Hamish drove up to the bungalow – his police Land Rover having been returned to him by Strathbane headquarters – Alison had turned Priscilla in her mind into a scheming harpy.

'Won't you come in for a cup of coffee?' she asked.

'No, I'd best be getting home,' replied Hamish. 'See you tomorrow.'

He smiled and Alison suddenly felt elated and lighthearted.

'You asked *who* to teach ye to drive?' Mrs Todd had been in the act of whipping up a bowl of batter when Alison told her on the following day about the proposed driving lessons. She stood with her mouth slightly open, the wire whisk poised over the bowl. No modern electrical methods for Mrs Todd.

'I asked Hamish Macbeth and he agreed. I mean the local bobby is surely the best –'

'Him!' Mrs Todd put down bowl and spoon. 'Let me tell you that man is a womanizer. The things I've heard! He's lazy and incompetent and useless. Why, when my man died, he came around, poking his nose into everything.'

'But . . . but . . . I mean, the village *loves* him,' wailed Alison. 'You saw the reception.'

'Aye, and a waste o' time and money.' Mrs Todd was a formidable figure even in her early seventies; her hair was still brown and her back ramrod straight. Her eyes narrowed suddenly. 'Are you sure Mrs Baird gave ye permission to take that car of hers out?'

'Yes,' said Alison in a shrill voice. 'And now I had better get back to typing out Mrs Baird's autobiography.'

'I'd like to read that,' said Mrs Todd, momentarily diverted. 'She's a fine lady and has travelled a lot.'

'You can ask her for a look at it when she gets back,' said Alison, wondering what on earth Mrs Todd would think of Maggie's explicitly described sexual adventures.

But Alison did not type that day; she read and reread the Highway Code, occasionally looking up at the clock to check the time and to will it to pass more quickly.

Promptly at six o'clock, Hamish drew up in the police Land Rover. To Alison's relief, Mrs Todd had left for the day.

Alison had already opened the garage doors. Hamish stood looking at the Renault. 'It's a grand wee car,' he said. 'But I think before the test, we'd better let Ian down at the garage have a look at it. If there's anything at all up with your car, they won't even let you start the test. Are you ready? Get in the driving seat. You'll be starting right away.'

Alison climbed in and Hamish doubled his lanky length into the passenger seat beside her.

'Now,' he said, 'check that your seat is the right distance from the pedals and that you don't have to stretch. And then check your driving mirrors.'

Alison shuffled about, jerking the car seat up too far forward and then sending it flying too far back in her excitement. Hamish got out again and took two Learner plates out of the Land Rover and fixed them to the front and back windows of the Renault.

He climbed in again and then began to instruct Alison how to move off. 'Mirror, signal, then manoeuvre,' he said. 'You turn your head and take a quick look back before you move off. Just imagine you're out on a busy road. Turn on the engine, put the gear into first, release the clutch slowly to the biting point, that is until you feel the car surge forward a bit, and then release the handbrake.'

Alison stalled several times. How could she ever get the coordination right? Driving was an unnatural act.

'I think we'll change places for a bit,' said Hamish, 'and I'll take ye out on the road. Hardly anyone about at this time of night.'

He patiently explained everything all over again once they were out on the road while Alison, once more in the driver's seat, prayed to the God in whom she did not believe to send her wisdom.

And then suddenly she was moving slowly along the cliff road while Hamish's patient voice told her when to change gear – and then she was driving, the headlamps cutting a magic path through the night. Hamish decided to let her drive straight along for as long as possible to give her confidence. It was too early to teach her how to reverse or park. Alison, maintaining a nervous 30 m.p.h., felt she was flying as free as the wind.

At last Hamish suggested gently that he turn the car and take her home.

To Alison, Hamish Macbeth had become a godlike figure. She was so grateful to him and so shy of him at the same time, she could hardly stammer out an offer of coffee. But Hamish Macbeth was cautious and old-fashioned and knew enough about village gossip to realize that even in this isolated spot, someone would somehow find out he had gone into the house with Miss Alison Kerr and so he refused.

He was surprised the following night to find a much more confident Alison, but Alison explained she had been driving up and down the short driveway all day. And then just as she was cruising along the cliff road, the engine began to cough and then died completely. 'It's Maggie, that old bitch,' shouted Alison. 'She's been mistreating this car for years.'

'Now, now,' said Hamish soothingly. 'I'll just hae a look under the bonnet.'

Alison waited in an agony of suspense while

he raised the bonnet and examined the engine under the light of a powerful torch.

He came back shaking his head. 'Ian'll need to hae a look at it,' he said. 'Wait here and I'll walk back and get the Land Rover and we'll tow it down to Lochdubh. Have you any money?'

'I've been collecting my dole money,' said Alison, 'and I've quite a bit.'

'Fine. Repairs are expensive, although I'll have a word wi' Ian. He owes me a few favours.'

Ian Chisholm, the garage owner-cum-repairman, was not pleased at having to work after hours, and grumbled at the filthy state of the engine. 'I'll dae ma best,' he said at last. 'But it'll cost ye. The points need cleaning and while ye're at it, it needs a new clutch plate.'

'A wee word with you, Ian,' said Hamish, leading him away from Alison.

Alison waited anxiously while the two men put their heads together.

Then they shook hands and Ian came back with a false sort of smile on his monkey face. 'Aye, weel, Miss Kerr, it seems it won't cost that much. Hamish'll pick up yer car the morrow.'

Later that night, Hamish got out his fishing tackle and set off in the driving rain to poach a salmon, praying that the water bailiffs wouldn't catch him. The salmon was in part payment for the car repairs. He did not get home until three in the morning. He put an eighteen-pound salmon on the kitchen table and went thankfully to bed after giving Towser a good rub down, for the dog had accompanied him on his poaching expedition.

Damn Alison Kerr, was his last waking thought, that lassie fair gives me the creeps.

Colonel Halburton-Smythe rustled his morning paper and looked over it at his daughter's calm face. She was reading letters that had arrived for her in that morning's post.

'Looks as if we're about to have a marriage in Lochdubh,' said the colonel.

'Mmm?' said Priscilla absently.

'Yes, that *friend* of yours, that Hamish Macbeth, has been courting Mrs Baird's niece, or we all hope that's what he's been doing. He's been up at the bungalow every night.'

'Oh, yes,' said Priscilla absently. 'Nice for him,' and she continued to read her letters.

The colonel gave her bent head a pleased smile. He had been wrong. His daughter quite obviously had no romantic interest in that lazy village copper.

What on earth is Hamish playing at? thought Priscilla furiously, he can surely do better than get tied up with that little drip. He's probably sorry for her. Typical Hamish! He'll probably end up tied down for life to some dowdy female just because he's sorry for her. She picked up her letters and walked slowly from the room. She had called at the police station several evenings in a row but Hamish had always been out.

She looked at the clock. Ten in the morning. She was due to leave for London at the weekend. She'd better find out what Hamish was thinking about, fooling around with Alison Kerr.

She drove down to the police station, but although the Land Rover was parked outside, there was no sign of Hamish. She peered in the living room window. Towser was stretched out on the sofa, his eyes closed.

Now, if I were Hamish, thought Priscilla, where would I be at this time in the morning without dog or car? She stood for a moment. Small flakes of snow were beginning to fall. Her face cleared. He was probably at the Lochdubh Hotel, mooching coffee.

And that is exactly where she did run Hamish to earth. He was sitting in the manager's office, a mug of steaming coffee in his hands.

He rose in pleased surprise as Priscilla walked in. 'I thought you would be back in London,' said Hamish.

'Not till the weekend,' said Priscilla. 'Morning, Mr Johnson. I just wanted a quick word with Hamish.'

'I've got to get back to work,' said the hotel manager. 'Be my guest, Miss Halburton-Smythe. Help yourself to coffee.'

'No, not here,' said Priscilla.

'Is it police business?' asked Hamish anxiously.

'Something like that.'

They walked together to the police station, Priscilla refusing to discuss what was bothering her until they were both indoors.

'It's like this,' she said, not looking at him. 'I've been hearing tales that you are courting Alison Kerr.'

He studied her averted face and a flash of malice appeared in his eyes. 'I had tae get interested in someone sometime,' he said softly.

'Just so long as you're really interested in her and not just sorry for her,' said Priscilla.

'Well, that iss verra kind of you, Miss Halburton-Smythe. I am glad I haff your blessing. Alison is all for a white wedding and I suppose I'll just haff to go along with it.'

Priscilla sat down at the table. Towser put his heavy head on her lap and she absentmindedly stroked his ears.

Her face was quite expressionless. Hamish looked at her thoughtfully and remembered the days when he would have given his back teeth for some sign of jealousy from Priscilla. He was glad he was not in love with her any more, but he valued her friendship, he told himself, and even dressed as she was that morning in tweed skirt and blouse with an old oilskin coat thrown over them, she looked very beautiful. Her bright hair almost hid her face as she bent over the dog.

He sighed and sat down at the table next to her. 'I am pulling your leg, Priscilla,' he said. 'Alison has been getting driving lessons from me. That lassie's obsessed with driving. She eats, sleeps, and drinks driving. I'm pretty sure that aunt of hers never gave her permission to use the car, but that's her problem.'

'I suppose she's an interesting girl?' remarked Priscilla slowly.

'Meaning that someone as plain as that must have something going for her? Shame on you, Priscilla.'

'I didn't mean that at all,' said Priscilla, raising her head at last.

'She must be in her thirties but away from the driving wheel, she's scared o' her own shadow,' said Hamish. 'I wish I'd never agreed to teach her. She clings to me, like a limpet, emotionally, I mean. I can feel her sticky presence even when she isn't here. She's got a crush on me . . . for the moment. She's a walking parasite on the perpetual lookout for a host.'

'Hamish!' exclaimed Priscilla, torn between relief that he was still heart free and amazement at his unexpected cruelty.

'I sound awful, don't I? But there's something unhealthy about her. I feel like swatting her with a fly swatter. It's not that she physically clings to me – she *mentally* clings and even when she's not about, I can feel that sticky mind of hers fantasizing about me.'

'Really, Hamish Macbeth, are you not getting a little bit carried away? Your vanity might be prompting you into thinking she fancies you.'

'Perhaps,' said Hamish with a disarming smile. 'Now when I'm interested, really interested in a lassie, I wouldnae know if she had a fancy for me or not unless she threw herself into my arms.'

But you are no longer interested in me, thought Priscilla, rather bleakly. Aloud, she said, 'Where's Maggie Baird gone?'

'I think she's gone to get herself beautified. Think it possible?'

'Hard to imagine,' said Priscilla. 'Is there some fellow about? Is that what caused the attack at the party? Did she see some old lover in the crowd? There were a few guests from England at the Lochdubh Hotel who joined in the festivities.'

'I've been thinking about that,' said Hamish, stretching out his long legs. 'I think she saw nobody but herself.'

'Oh, Hamish, no one finds their own appearance such a shock.'

'Not people like you. But just imagine if she had let herself go to seed but carried around in her head the image of what she used to be like. And then suddenly she saw herself in all her glory.'

'Could be. I remember a fashion buyer at a store in London saying that because most of their customers were middle-aged and plump, they decided to use plump middle-aged models. It was a disaster. The buyer said she found out that when a woman buys a gown she's seen on a young and pretty model, she sees herself a little bit as that model. Interesting psychology. I'd better be going.'

'Are you driving down to London?'

'No, only to Inverness. There's too much fog on the motorways at this time of year. I get the train at eight in the morning. When is Alison's driving test?'

'Time's passed quickly. It's this Friday morning.'

'Well, good luck with your pupil. Bye, Hamish. See you in the summer.'

'Bye.' He kissed her cheek and for a moment she felt his face, unexpectedly smooth, against her own. She gave a little ducking motion of her head and turned and left the police station.

The day of Alison's driving test dawned sunny and fair, with a white frost rapidly melting from the roads and heathland. The sea loch sparkled and shimmered with light and the little eighteenth-century cottages strung out along the waterfront looked neat and picturesque. The distorted giant shapes of the Two Sisters, the mountains which dominated the village, were covered with snow. The air was redolent with the smells of a West Highland village – wood smoke, fish, tar, and strong tea.

As Hamish drove Alison into the village, he

saw the examiner standing outside the hotel and muttered, 'Oh, dear.'

'What did you say?' demanded Alison sharply.

'Nothing,' lied Hamish. But he had recognized the examiner, nicknamed The Beast of Strathbane, Frank Smeedon. But better not tell Alison that. Smeedon had been off work for some months and his replacement had been a kindly, cheery man. Poor Alison, thought Hamish bleakly.

'Now just keep calm and do your best,' he told Alison.

He could not bear to watch the start of the test but strolled off along the waterfront. Alison would be away for half an hour. He went into the Lochdubh Hotel and into the manager's office.

'You've got a face like a fiddle,' said Mr Johnson.

'I've just dropped Alison off for her driving test and the examiner is Smeedon.'

'Oh, my, my, she hasnae a hope in hell,' said Mr Johnson. 'That man hates wee lassies.'

'It's her own fault for looking like a waif,' muttered Hamish. 'She's in her thirties. Why is he such a woman hater? He's married, isn't he?'

'Aye, he's not only married, he's got a bint on the side.'

'Neffer!' exclaimed Hamish. 'Who?'

'D'ye ken that driving school in Strathbane, Harrison's? Well, there's a secretary there, a little blonde tart. He's old enough tae be her father.'

'What's her name?'

'Maisie MacCallum.'

'And does Mrs Smeedon know about this?'

'No, she's an auld battleaxe, and she'd kill him if she ever found out. Coffee, Hamish?'

'No, it's a grand day. Think I'll chust stretch my legs. In fact, I haff neffer seen a better day.'

Mr Johnson, like Priscilla, had known Hamish long enough to recognize the danger signals in the sudden sibilancy of Hamish's Highland accent.

'Hey!' said Mr Johnson in alarm. 'What I told you about Smeedon is in confidence!'

But Hamish had gone.

Alison was meanwhile feeling calm and confident. She had driven correctly along single-track roads, she had reversed competently and performed a three-point turn with exact precision. She sat in the car and correctly answered all Mr Smeedon's questions on the Highway Code. When he snapped his notebook shut and picked up his clipboard, she smiled at him, waiting for the tremendous news that she had passed.

'Well, ye've failed,' said the examiner.

Alison's world came tumbling about her ears. Failure again. 'What did I do wrong?' she asked in a shaky voice.

'Not allowed to tell ye,' he said smugly.

'But that's not true! All that's been changed. I read in the paper that examiners –' began

Alison desperately. There was a rap at the window on the driving instructor's side. Smeedon looked up and saw Hamish Macbeth.

'Good day to ye, Miss Kerr,' said Smeedon, opening the door and getting out. Alison laid her head on the steering wheel and wept.

'Good morning, Mr Smeedon,' said Hamish lazily. 'Spring won't be far off and the thoughts of men will turn to love. But of course in your case, they've already turned.'

'Blethering idiot,' snapped Smeedon, beginning to stride towards his own car. Hamish put out a long arm and held Smeedon's shoulder in a strong grip. 'I'm not asking ye if Miss Kerr passed her test,' said Hamish, 'for you were determined to fail her before she even got behind the wheel. Whit hae ye got against the lassies? I wonder what Maisie MacCallum would say if she knew what you were really like?'

Smeedon looked as if he had been struck by lightning. His face took on a grey tinge. Like quite a lot of first-time philanderers, he was convinced his doings were immune from the probings of prying eyes.

'You wouldnae dare,' he breathed.

'I'm a verra kindly man,' said Hamish, 'but I hate injustice and that Alison Kerr is a champion driver – everything exactly by the book. Now if I thought you'd failed her out o' spite, there's no knowing what I'd do. They've been complaints about ye before but always from failed drivers and it was probably put down to disappointment on their part. But what if a policeman were to add his voice to the complaints? And what if that self-same policeman were a verra moral fellow and decided Mrs Smeedon ought to know what you were up to . . .?'

'I passed Miss Kerr,' said Smeedon desperately.

'You told her?'

'Aye, well I was thinking of something else and made a wee mistake.'

'Just you stand there and write out that she's passed and that'll be an end o' the matter,' said Hamish.

The examiner rapidly scribbled out a form that stated that Alison Kerr had passed her driving test. Hamish twitched it out of his fingers. 'Now off with you,' he said sternly.

'You'll not . . .?'

'No, I won't be saying a word to Mrs Smeedon,' said Hamish, but, as the examiner scurried to his car, he added softly, 'but that complaint about you failing people out o' spite is going in just the same.'

He went over to the Renault, opened the door, and slid into the passenger seat.

'Here,' he said, holding out Alison's pass form, 'dry your eyes wi' this.'

Alison took it blindly and then blinked down at it through her thick glasses. She stared at it. Then she scrubbed her eyes under her glasses with her sopping handkerchief and looked again.

'But he said I'd failed.'

'We all make mistakes,' said Hamish comfortably. 'He's put it right.'

Alison flung her arms around him and pressed a damp kiss against his cheek. 'You did this,' she said in a choked voice. 'You made him do it.'

'Now, now,' said Hamish, pulling free and resisting a strong temptation to wipe his cheek with the back of his hand. 'Never mind who did or said what. You're free to drive on your own.'

Alison looked at him shyly. 'It's nearly lunch time,' she said, 'and I booked a table for us at the hotel . . . you know, for a celebration lunch. My little surprise.'

'That's very nice,' said Hamish, 'but I am on duty.'

'But *Hamish*!' Alison had dreamt about this lunch since she first thought of the idea.

Hamish opened the door and got out. How sweet the air outside was! It was as if Alison had been wearing a cloying sticky perfume although she never wore scent. 'Take yourself for a drive and enjoy yourself,' said Hamish, bending down and looking in at her. 'Oh, and get a photocopy of that form and then send it off to the DVLC and you should get your licence back through the post in a couple of weeks' time.' And before Alison could say any more, Hamish closed the car door and strolled off.

It was as well for Hamish that Alison was more obsessed with driving than she was with him or she would have chased after him. She sat rather bleakly, watching him in the driving mirror. Then she looked again at that pass form and a slow glow of sheer happiness spread through her body. She was free! She could drive anywhere she liked. The sun was sparkling and the road in front of her curved along the waterfront, over a humpbacked bridge and up the hill out of Lochdubh.

She switched on the engine and moved off. A car hooted and swept past her and the driver shouted something out of the window. She slammed on the brakes and sat shaking. She had forgotten to signal. She had even forgotten to check her mirrors or look around.

She tried to move off again, but the car would not budge. She switched the engine off again and covered her face with her hands. Think! Then she slowly removed her hands from her face and looked down at the hand-brake. She had forgotten to release it.

There was no Hamish beside her now to prompt her.

She squared her shoulders, switched on the engine again, moved into first gear, checked her mirrors, signalled, took a quick look over her shoulder and moved off slowly. By the time she had reached the top of the road leading out of Lochdubh, she had to pull on to the side of the road to flex her hands which had pins and needles caused by her terrified grip on the wheel.

'This will never do,' she said aloud.

She started off again. The road was quiet. No cars behind her and none coming the other way. Slowly, she increased her speed until she was bowling along, her hands relaxed on the wheel, but only dimly aware of the stupendous majesty of the Sutherland mountains soaring on either side of the road. She drove on and on, down past the Kyles of Sutherland and the towns of Bonar Bridge and Ardgay and then up the famous Struie Pass – famous for being a motorist's nightmare – but Alison did not know that and put her fear down to her own inexperience. The road climbed and climbed, seeming almost perpendicular and then she was running along the pass through the top of the mountains and finally down and down the twisting hairpin bends towards the Cromarty Firth which lay sparkling and glinting in the pale sunlight.

Alison came to a roundabout. A road went on over a mile-long bridge towards Inverness. On the other side of the roundabout lay the road to Dingwall. Dingwall sounded like a smaller town and therefore one with manageable traffic. She went round the roundabout and realized as she took the Dingwall road that she had forgotten to signal. All her nervousness returned.

She parked in one of the tiny town's surprisingly many car parks, choosing a space well away from other cars and spending quite twenty minutes reversing the Renault into a space that could comfortably have held three trucks.

She carefully locked up and went down to the main street to look at the shops. She stopped by a phone box and, on impulse, went in and phoned the police station in Lochdubh. There was no reply. Then Alison noticed the light was fading fast. She had a long way to drive back. She headed back towards the car park, feeling in her pocket for the car keys.

Where the keys should have been was a large hole.

Alison stopped dead. She felt sick. She retraced her steps, scanning the ground. But Dingwall should receive an award for being the cleanest town in Britain – they *vacuum* the streets. There wasn't even a scrap of paper.

She stopped someone and asked directions to the police station.

The police station was not at all like Hamish's cosy village quarters. It was a large modern building with a plaque on the wall stating that the foundation stone had been laid by Princess Alexandria. She pushed open the door and went in.

A fey-looking girl was standing at the reception desk, chain-smoking.

'My keys,' Alison blurted out. 'I've lost my car keys.'

'We've got them,' said the girl, lighting a fresh cigarette off the stub of the old one. 'Just been handed in.' And then she stood looking at Alison through the curling cigarette smoke.

'Oh, that's wonderful.' Alison felt limp with relief. 'I'll just take them.'

'You can't get them till Monday,' replied the girl.

'Monday! This is Friday afternoon. Monday!'

'You see that door behind me?' The girl indicated a door behind her and a little to the right which was like a house door with a large letter box. 'Well, the found stuff gets put through that letter box where it falls down to the bottom of a wire cage on the other side. The person who has the key to the door has gone off for a long week-end.'

'But someone else must have the key,' said Alison, her voice taking on the shrill note of the coward trying to be assertive.

'No,' said the Highland maiden patiently. 'Only one person has the key. You see,' she went on with mad logic, 'if anything goes missing, we've only the one person to blame.'

Alison's lips trembled. 'I want my keys.'

'I'll see if the sergeant can do anything.' The girl stubbed out her cigarette and disappeared. After a few moments, the sergeant came back with her. Again Alison told her story and again heard the tale of the one person with the key.

'But I live in Lochdubh. I must get home.' Alison was becoming terrified. What if Maggie should phone or, even worse, turn up in person?

'Now, now, we'll do our best.' He called into the back of the police station and another policeman, seemingly of more senior rank, appeared.

'Och, I think we can help you,' he said, and then as Alison watched, he took off his tunic and rolled up his sleeves. The sergeant produced a wire coat hanger which he proceeded to unravel, and then both policemen began to *fish* down the letter box, rather like schoolboys fishing down a drain and with as many chuckles, and 'a wee bit mair tae yer right, Frank,' and other jolly words of encouragement.

After half an hour – the Highland police force has endless patience – the door to the police station opened and a young man rushed in. He had hair *en brosse*, a gold earring, and a desperate expression on his face. He tried to get attention but failed because the policemen were too busy fishing.

Control yourself, said Alison's inner voice. It's not the end of the world. It's only car keys. This poor man looks as if he's here to report a murder. Aloud, she said to the young man. 'Ring the bell on the wall.'

He did and the sergeant turned reluctantly from the letter box. 'What do you want?'

'Can I use your toilet?' asked the young man.

'Sure. Through there.'

'This is madness!' howled Alison. 'Look, give me the address of whoever has the key and I will take a taxi there and pick it up.'

'It's twenty miles out on the Black Isle.'

'I don't care,' said Alison, tears of frustration standing out in her eyes.

'Och, you English are always that impatient,' said the sergeant with a grin. 'But we've got things in hand. We've sent out for a magnet.'

The girl of the reception and the cigarettes had returned. 'A magnet!' said Alison. The girl avoided her eyes and pretended to read some papers.

Another half-hour passed by while night fell outside and Alison tried not to scream at the forces of law and order and then suddenly a cheer went up. 'Got 'em!'

'There you are,' said the sergeant. 'There was nothing for you to get upset about, now was there?'

But ungrateful Alison simply snatched the keys out of his hand and ran out without a word of thanks.

Her face tense under the glare of the sodium street lights, she walked back through the deserted streets to the car park. Dingwall, like most Highland towns, had closed down for the night. No one will believe this, she thought, it's cloud cuckoo land.

She got into the car, switched on the lights, and began the long drive home. Night driving was misery to Alison. Approaching headlamps seemed to draw her like a moth and she kept having to twitch the wheel nervously to make sure she kept to the correct side of the road. By the time she finally parked in Lochdubh and got out of the car, her legs were trembling and she was afraid she would fall.

She rang the police station bell but Hamish had seen her coming and was lying down behind his living room sofa, waiting for her to go away.

Sadly, Alison went home. It had been a nightmare. Driving was a nightmare. She would never get back behind the wheel again.

But no sooner had she managed to park the car neatly in the garage than she found herself already restless for a new day, a day that would contain her two favourite obsessions – driving and Hamish Macbeth.

Priscilla climbed aboard the Highland Chieftain, the train which was to take her from Inverness to London. Outside the snow had begun to fall and inside, the air conditioning was blasting away. She had complained before about the freezing temperature on British Rail trains and so knew she had no chance of getting any heat. She wondered savagely if the anti-pollution campaigners had thought of doing anything about British Rail. The employees, reflected Priscilla, were so bloody rude that most people preferred to drive and pollute the air rather than go by train. It was rather like entering a Kafkaesque state where ordinary laws, rules, and courtesies did not apply. The motto of British Rail should be

'Sod the Public,' thought Priscilla, standing up to get down a travelling case and find an extra sweater.

She sat down again and looked out of the window and there, strolling along the platform, came Hamish Macbeth. She waved to him and he climbed aboard the train and handed her a travelling rug. 'Thought you might be cold,' he said.

'Oh, Hamish, how sweet of you!' Priscilla put the rug over her knees. 'Did you come all this way just to see me off?'

'Och, no, I haff the police business in Inverness.'

'And what police business do you have that the Inverness police cannot cope with?'

'It's a secret,' said Hamish stiffly. 'Have a good trip and I will be seeing you in the summer.'

He turned about and marched off the train.

I've offended him, thought Priscilla miserably, of course he wouldn't come just to see me off but even if he did, I shouldn't have said so. Then she noticed the travelling rug was thickly covered in dog hairs and it also smelt of dog. Poor Towser. Priscilla stroked the blanket. I hope he doesn't miss his rug too much.

Hamish walked angrily out of the station. What on earth had made him drive all the way to Inverness just to say goodbye to Priscilla? The fact was, he suddenly thought, stopping dead in his tracks and oblivious to curious stares, he missed being in love with her. He had only been hoping to stir up a few embers. And imagine giving away poor old Towser's favourite rug.

'Better buy the smelly mongrel a new one,' he said aloud, 'or he'll be mad at me for weeks.'

He looked down and found a small middle-aged woman looking up at him curiously.

'Can I help you, madam?' he demanded, awfully.

The woman sniffed and then said, 'I'm thinking ye could do wi' a bit o' help yersel', laddie, staunin' there mumbling.'

Hamish walked on, pink with irritation.

Damn all women!

Chapter Four

I'd be a butterfly; living like a rover,
Dying when fair things are fading away.
                                    – T.H. Bayly

Spring comes late to the highlands, turning
Sutherland into a blue and misty landscape;
light blue rain-washed skies, far away mountains of a darker blue, cobalt blue sea.

And always through the glory of the awak-
ening world drove Alison Kerr, propelled by
her obsession with the car. She kept away from
Hamish Macbeth, being of the timid nature
which prefers love long distance. It was all too
easy to understand he was not interested in her
when she was with him; but easy to dream that
he really was in love with her after all when he
was absent.

So Alison was happier than she had ever
been in her life. There was the magnificent
stark beauty of Sutherland, the car, the cosy,
practical mothering of Mrs Todd, the car,
Hamish Macbeth, the car, no Maggie, and the
car, which she had come to regard as her own.

She privately called the car 'Rover', imagining it to be like a faithful and affectionate dog.

And then as spring gave way to early summer and great splashes of bell heather coloured the mountains and the nights were long and light, those northern nights where it hardly ever gets really dark, back into this paradise came Maggie Baird, although no one, not even Alison, recognized her at first.

She was svelte and beautiful with golden hair in a soft, clever style and a wardrobe of clothes by Jean Muir. She had high cheekbones and her eyes were large and very blue. She walked into the kitchen where Alison was having coffee with Mrs Todd and stood for a moment, relishing the dawning surprise on both faces.

'Yes, it's me,' she said triumphantly, if ungrammatically.

'It can't be,' breathed Alison. 'I wouldn't have known you. What have you done to yourself?'

'Best health farm and best plastic surgeon,' said Maggie, who had also acquired a new husky voice. 'Gosh, it's good to be back in Peasantville. Take my coat, Mrs Todd. I'm expecting four guests tomorrow so I want you to get the beds ready. Hang that coat up and come back and I'll tell you about it.'

Alison looked at the beautiful Maggie in a dazed way. Maggie, she reflected, was like a highly coloured butterfly that had emerged from a chrysalis of fat. Then sharp anguish struck Alison around the region of the midriff. The car! What would happen to her driving?

'Who are these four guests?' she asked instead.

'They are four fellows I used to know,' said Maggie, stretching and yawning. 'I've decided the single state doesn't suit me so I went through my old lists and came up with four who are likely to propose. There's Peter Jenkins, he's an advertising executive, Crispin Witherington who owns a car sales room in Finchley, James Frame who runs a gambling club, and that pop singer, Steel Ironside.'

'I thought he was dead,' said Alison.

'Who?'

'Steel Ironside. He hasn't made a record in years.'

'He's alive, all right.'

'And you expect one of them to propose to you just like that?'

Maggie smiled slowly while Alison studied her aunt's new face for wrinkles and couldn't find one. 'I expect all of them to propose. Oh, I don't rate my charms all that much. They all need money and whichever one marries me will get it and so I'll tell 'em. Cuts you out, of course.'

'How does it cut me out?' asked Alison.

'Oh, I'd made my will out in your favour but I'll change it as soon as I've made my choice.'

'How's your heart?' asked Alison and then blushed.

'Hoping I'll pop off before I change my will? Hard luck, sweetie.'

Mrs Todd came back and Maggie began to tell her briskly what to do about preparing for the guests. If only Maggie *would* drop dead, thought Alison fiercely, it would all be mine, the house and the car and Mrs Todd.

She longed for Hamish. In fact the only thing to lighten her misery at Maggie's return was that it gave her a good excuse to visit Hamish. But, oh, that dreadfully long, long walk along the coast now that she could not use the car.

'Have you finished typing that manuscript for me?' Alison suddenly realized Maggie was speaking to her.

'Yes, it's all typed up,' said Alison, quickly averting her eyes so that Maggie should not see the disgust in them. The manuscript had become increasingly pornographic as it went along. Until she had read Maggie's book, Alison, who read a great deal, had thought that she knew every sexual kink and aberration there was, but Maggie's writing had introduced her to a whole new and disgusting world of sleaze. Then Alison decided to take the plunge. Better to ask Maggie about the car, this new and relaxed Maggie, and to ask her while Mrs Todd was present.

'I've a surprise for you, Maggie,' she said in a breathless rush. 'I passed my driving test while you were away.' The words began to tumble out. It wasn't Mrs Todd's fault. She,

Alison, had told her that she had had Maggie's permission to use the car, but Alison knew that dear Maggie wouldn't really mind because . . .

Her voice trailed away before the glacial expression in Maggie's now beautiful and large blue eyes.

'That is *my* car,' said Maggie, 'and you are not to touch it again, d'ye hear? Now I am going down to the village to stun them all with my new appearance. I may even drop in and try my hand with that copper, and while I'm gone, I suggest you start earning your keep by helping Mrs Todd with the preparations.'

She strode out, tottering slightly on her very high heels.

A few minutes later, there came the harsh sound of revving from the garage. Alison crossed to the kitchen window and looked out.

Maggie drove out of the garage. The entrance to the bungalow garden was narrow and flanked by two gateposts. As Alison watched, Maggie scraped the car along one of the gateposts on her way out. Alison let out a whimper of pain as if the car were a pet dog which was being tormented.

Mrs Todd's calm Scottish voice sounded behind her. 'I think we'd better be getting on with our work, Miss Kerr. I do not need the help but it would be as well to keep herself happy on her first day back.'

Alison moved through the housework, feeling as though she were one mass of pain. That precious car that she had polished and waxed and oiled! Tears began to run down her face. She prayed to all the gods to strike Maggie Baird down.

'Come on now, lassie,' said Mrs Todd. 'If I was you, I would be getting the local papers and looking for a wee job. Take ye out o' the house until you get on your feet.'

'How can I take a local job when I haven't a car?' sobbed Alison.

'If ye're that desperate,' said Mrs Todd grimly, 'ye'll walk. It's only fifteen miles to the village.'

But fifteen miles to town-bred Alison seemed impossible. She had done it once to go to ask Hamish about driving lessons. But to do it every day!

It comes as quite a shock to the respectable female to find that quite ordinary and decent-looking men frequent tarts. When Alison first met Maggie's four guests she was surprised to find that, with the exception of the failed pop singer, they all looked normal and ordinary. The fact that Maggie, in the old days, had been what would have been called a high flyer or good-time girl did not cut any ice with Alison. She had read Maggie's manuscript and knew what she had got up to between the sheets – or in the woods, or up against walls, or on yachts – and did not realize that Maggie's less exotic liaisons had all been pretty normal and regular.

Crispin Witherington, the owner of the car sales room, was middle-aged, like the others. He had that glossy artificial look which comes from a lot of gin and saunas. He was slightly balding, with black restless eyes, a small button of a nose, and a prim little mouth. He was expensively if tastelessly dressed, his double-breasted blazer with some impossible crest draped across his stomach and the flowered handkerchief in his breast pocket matching his flowered tie.

James Frame, from the gambling club, was tall and willowy and rabbity looking. He had a strangulated voice and appeared to cultivate a 'silly ass' manner which he fondly imagined to be upper class. He had patent leather hair and smelled strongly of expensive aftershave.

The pop singer remained frozen in the age of Sergeant Pepper. He had grey shoulder-length hair, small half-moon glasses, a denim jacket and jeans, a flowered waistcoat with watch chain, and red leather shoes. He spoke with a strong Liverpudlian accent, nasal and irritating to the ear and somehow slightly phony as if he had adopted it during the Beatles era.

Finally, the advertising man, Peter Jenkins, was tall and fair with a thin, clever, rather weak face and a drawling voice. In normal circumstances, Alison would have been impressed by him, but as it was, Maggie's bedroom antics came between her and her assessment of the four men although not one of them had featured in the memoirs.

The men all talked about their surprise at getting Maggie's invitation and how marvellous she looked, while Maggie flirted and cajoled and flattered, exuding that air of maternal warmth that she seemed able to turn on at will. They all, with the exception of Maggie who had a salad and Alison who was too distressed to feel hungry, ate their way through an enormous meal.

It was when they were sitting over coffee after dinner that Maggie casually announced that she wanted to get married again and that any husband of hers would find himself a very rich man, 'and probably sooner than he thinks,' said Maggie, one hand fluttering to her bosom. 'Got this terrible dicky heart.'

It was all very neat, thought Alison, sensing the sudden stillness in the room. Maggie had said it all. She was rich and she hadn't long to live. Then the conversation became general as the men began to reminisce about old friends and acquaintances.

Maggie was the centre of attention. She was wearing a clinging dinner gown in a soft material. It was smoky blue and she was wearing a fine sapphire and diamond necklace. The skirt of the gown was folded over so that when she sat, she revealed one long leg encased in a gossamer fine stocking. Her breasts, expertly reduced in size, were displayed to advantage by the low neck of the gown. She was playful, she was amusing, she was teasing, and she threw only a few barbed remarks in Alison's direction. But she did order Alison around. 'Fetch Peter a drink,' or, 'Move that ashtray nearer Crispin.'

But as the evening wore on, the tension in the air grew, and the men, with the exception of Peter Jenkins, the advertising executive, began to vie for Maggie's attention. Maggie persuaded Steel to get his guitar and perform. The pop singer returned with an electric guitar. While he was singing what seemed to be a protest song, Maggie began to tear up little pieces of paper napkin and pass them around to the other three men to use as earplugs. Fortunately for Steel, he was too absorbed in his performance to notice his audience was sniggering. Alison found it all very unpleasant. Her head ached. She mourned her lost days of freedom. She hadn't been able to bear to look at the car when Maggie had brought it home, a Maggie full of stories about how Hamish Macbeth had called her 'a miracle'.

The guests, fortunately, were tired after their journeys and an early night was proposed. Fully dressed, Alison lay in bed, waiting until she heard the large bungalow settling into silence. Then she rose and put on her coat and went downstairs and out to the garage. She opened the small side door, switched on the light and stood looking at the little red car. There was a vicious scrape along the right side. Alison began to cry in a dreary, hopeless sort of way. She had to get away from Maggie, but how could she find the strength to make the first move?

She heard steps crunch on the gravel and switched off the light and walked outside. A tall dark figure stood outside the house, watching her.

'Who is it?' asked Alison, her voice barely above a whisper.

'Peter Jenkins.'

'What do you want?'

'Just need to get some air.' He moved closer, sensing rather than seeing her distress. 'You upset about something?'

'It's the car,' whimpered Alison. 'She scraped the car.'

'Maggie did? I don't understand. Is it your car?'

'No.'

There was a long silence.

Then Peter let out a faint sigh. 'I don't want to go back in there yet. I may as well hear your troubles. Come and sit in *my* car and tell me all about it.'

'I'll bore you,' said Alison.

'More than likely. But come along anyway.'

His car turned out to be the latest model of Jaguar. It was parked with the others in a bit of open space outside the gateposts. He turned on the engine and switched on the heater. 'It'll get warm pretty quickly,' he said. 'Cigarette?'

'I can't,' said Alison. 'I've had cancer.' She began to sob and hiccup again.

He handed her a handkerchief and waited for her to stop, then gently urged her to tell her story. Bit by bit it all came out. 'If only she would die,' said Alison. 'She's going to change her will as soon as she chooses one of you as a husband.'

'She can't choose me,' said Peter. 'I don't want her.'

'Why was she so sure of you, then?'

The end of Peter's cigarette glowed red in the darkness as he dragged on it. Then he said, 'She's changed. I had a fling with her, oh, let me see, I'm forty-eight now, say, about twenty years ago.'

'How did it start?' asked Alison, curious despite her misery. 'I mean, did you just say, I will pay you "X" amount to go to bed with me?'

'No, no, that's not how the Maggies of this world operate. We went out on dates, I fell in love, she appeared to. At first it was expensive restaurants and expensive holidays, then she needed help with her mortgage, then she needed some bills paid, then it seemed logical to besotted me to give her a weekly allowance. But on my part, it was all for love.'

'And then you got wise to her?'

'Oh, no, she ditched *me*, for an Arab sheik, and left for the south of France with him. It took me a long time to get over it. There's something cruel and, well . . . unbalanced about her now. I couldn't believe my luck when I got her letter. I didn't know she had

invited the other fellows. She used to be so
funny and warm and scatty and affectionate.
You couldn't help forgiving her. That's why I
couldn't sleep. I've been carrying a torch for
her for years. Never married. What a waste!'

But Alison couldn't imagine a loveable
Maggie and thought Peter a fool.

'I wish I could speak to Hamish,' she said in
a small voice.

'Who's Hamish?'

'The village policeman.'

'But, look here, you can't report Maggie for
scraping her own car!'

'No, it's not that, it's just that Hamish seems
to make things all right.'

'Well, as I can't sleep, I'll take you there.'

'But it's after midnight!'

'If he's a conscientious bobby, he won't
mind being woken up.'

'All right,' said Alison shyly, suddenly
elated at the idea of seeing Hamish while
being accompanied by this handsome man.
And Peter *did* seem handsome to Alison, who
did not notice the weakness in his face, having
a pretty weak character herself.

Hamish Macbeth, opening the kitchen door –
Alison had quickly learned that friends and
locals never used the front door – thought
wearily as he looked at the two faces, God help
us all if the meek do inherit the earth. He
tucked his shirt tail into his trousers. He had
been undressing for bed when he had heard
the knock at the door. 'Come in,' he said. 'I

am sure it must be something awfy important to get me out o' bed.' Towser stood beside his master, blinking sleepily in the light. He let out a low growl, sensing Hamish's dislike of Alison.

'Oh, *Hamish*,' Alison wailed and threw herself against his chest.

Peter noticed the way the policeman quickly put Alison away from him. Fat lot of sympathy she's going to get from him, he thought, feeling suddenly protective of Alison.

'Sit down,' said Hamish, 'and I'll fetch us a dram.'

Hamish, when he drank, preferred warm bottled beer. His sideboard contained only a bottle of twelve-year-old malt whisky, a Christmas present he had never broached. It seemed such a waste to open it now, but hospitality was hospitality and Alison, tiresome though she might be, might cheer up with a little whisky inside her.

He went back into the kitchen, carrying bottle and glasses, and poured three measures. 'Now,' said Hamish, 'begin at the beginning and go on to the end. I have had a visit from herself today. My! Isn't plastic surgery and bleach the wondrous thing? She was like one of thae film stars, ye know, she looked like beauty preserved rather than beauty reclaimed.'

Clutching her glass, Alison told the whole dismal story, of Maggie's will, of her plans to marry, of her damaging the car, and ended up

91

with, 'I can't have any respect for her, Hamish, not after having read her book.'

'What book?' asked Peter Jenkins sharply.

'She's written a book about her affairs and a nasty bit of pornography it is too,' said Alison. 'So what am I to do, Hamish?'

'I've told you before,' said Hamish quietly. 'Get away from her. You're a grown woman. You can earn your own money.'

'But . . . but . . . I'm still weak and what if the cancer comes back?'

'It's got more chance of coming back if you stay on with her and keep getting yourself into a state,' said Hamish.

Peter Jenkins eyed the policeman coldly. What sort of help and comfort was this? In fact, what sort of policeman was this? In Peter's mind, policemen should always be on duty and always be in uniform. Hamish was wearing a tartan shirt, an old pair of cavalry twill trousers, and had thrust his bare feet into carpet slippers. His red hair was tousled and his eyelashes were ridiculously long.

'That sort of advice,' said Peter, 'is very easy to dole out, but very hard to take.'

'But the lassie's in such misery, anything else would be better,' said Hamish patiently. 'What would you suggest?'

'I would suggest, Officer, that you have a word with Mrs Baird and tell her to be nicer to Alison.'

'For heffen's sake.' Hamish stifled a yawn. 'If Mrs Baird wants to play the wicked step-mother and Alison here is hellbent on playing Cinderella, I can't do anything about it.'

'Come along, Alison,' said Peter Jenkins sternly. 'There's no point in your staying here. If you ask me, it's all a great waste of time.'

'I couldnae agree wi' you more,' said Hamish sweetly. His hazel eyes mocked Peter. 'Och, if you ask me, this lassie's got nothing to complain about. You've got to pull yourself together, Alison, you've become a right wee moaning Minnie.'

Shocked and hurt, Alison stumbled to her feet. Peter put an arm about her shoulders.

'You despicable pillock!' he raged at Hamish. 'Don't you see she's had more than enough to bear?'

'Aw, go and boil your heid,' said Hamish with lazy insolence.

Peter almost dragged Alison from the police station. As he slammed the door behind them, Hamish leapt from his chair and stood with his ear pressed against the kitchen door. 'In future, Alison,' he heard Peter say firmly, 'you'd be better off coming to me for help.'

Hamish grinned. Well, let's hope that got Sir Galahad up on his high horse, he said to himself, nothing like a bit o' knight errantry to stiffen the weakest spine.

Perhaps because of Hamish's remarks, Alison tried again on the following morning to get Maggie's permission to use the car, and the resultant row sounded around the house. If Alison wanted a car that much, she could damn well buy one, said Maggie, ending up by calling her 'a useless drip'.

Alison was shuffling about the garden later that day, kicking the weeds, when Crispin Witherington approached. 'Couldn't help hearing the row,' he said.

He was dressed in what he fondly imagined suitable gear for the Highlands – lovat green cord breeches with green socks and brogues, tweed jacket, checked shirt, and a paisley cravat held in place by a large gold horseshoe. He had a rasping, rather hectoring voice, but Alison wanted sympathy.

'I hate Maggie,' she muttered.

'Oh, it's just her fun. I'll bet she's fond of you. Tell you what, I'll let you drive my roller.'

'I'm only used to the small car,' said Alison, looking longingly to where Crispin's white Rolls Royce was parked.

'Oh, come on, have a go.'

'All right,' said Alison, suddenly feeling like no end of a femme fatale. Peter had shown an interest in her and now here was Crispin.

'Better drive it out on to the road for you,' said Crispin. 'I'll look up the map first and pick a place to go.'

'I know practically all the places 'round here,' said Alison, but Crispin crackled open an ordinance survey map as if she had not spoken.

94

'Ah, let's try this place, Fern Bay, sounds pretty.'

'I know the road there,' said Alison eagerly.

'Now, then, girlie, just you drive and I'll navigate. Always go by the map, that's my motto.'

Alison drove off, nervously at first but then slowly gaining confidence. But it was to be her first experience of a back-seat driver, or rather, a front-seat one. 'Too fast,' he snapped. 'Slow down a bit.'

Alison dutifully slowed down to thirty miles per hour.

'We'll never get anywhere if you're going to crawl along,' he said after a few minutes. 'Turn off next left.'

'But that's not the road to –'

'I said, turn off,' he growled.

Alison reduced speed at the turn with a great crash of gears. 'No wonder Maggie won't let you drive,' jeered Crispin.

She slowed the big car to a halt, switched off the engine and carefully put on the handbrake, and turned to him. Enough was enough! 'Why did you want me to come out with you?' she demanded in a thin, shaky voice. 'I know all the roads around here and I don't care what your map says, this is a dead end.'

He let out a hearty laugh although his eyes were humourless. 'You ladies are always touchy about your driving. So, I'm wrong. There! I apologize. Friends?'

'Yes,' said Alison weakly.

'You see, we could be of great help to each other.'

'I don't see how ...'

'Maggie's fond of you.' He took out a thin gold cigarette case and extracted a cigarette. 'I know she bitches at you like hell but she must like you or she wouldn't have made out her will in your favour.'

'But that was before you ...'

'Before we all turned up? I think she's playing games. I think she don't want any of us. She's changed.'

'When did you ... erm ... meet her?'

'Ten years ago just after my marriage broke up. She came in to buy a car, a Jag, and I ended up paying for it and when our affair broke up, she sold it and bought that heap of trash she's driving around at the moment.'

'That was a very good car,' said Alison furiously, 'before *she* started mangling it.'

'Well, have it your way. Anyway, then she was fun. It cost me a bomb but it was a barrel of laughs while it lasted.' He put a pudgy hand on Alison's knee and squeezed it. 'We could get along fine, girlie. Looks to me as if you haven't had much of a life. I could show you a good time.'

'I would like to go home now,' said Alison, her voice coming out in a squeak.

'Not yet. It's a fine afternoon. Let's find this Fern Bay and have a few noggins.'

Alison hadn't the courage to stand up to him. But he had stopped navigating and criticizing her driving. Alison pulled up out-side Fern Bay's one pub, which was more of a shack. It was a dingy bar ornamented with posters warning crofters of the penalties to be incurred if they did not dip their sheep, an announcement of a Girl Guide rally of a few years back, and a notice saying that drink would not be served to minors. A row of small men in cloth caps leaned over the bar.

Alison felt herself beginning to blush. There were still pubs in the Highlands where the presence of a female was frowned on and she felt this was one of them.

A juke box in the corner was grinding out a seventies pop record, the sort of music which might sound catchy to someone stoned on pot, but to the clearheaded appeared a series of rhythmic thumps overtopped by a harsh voice yelling out unintelligible sounds.

Crispin approached the bar and squeezed his way in between two of the locals. 'Hey, mine host,' he cried. 'A little service here.'

'Aye, whit dae ye want?' said the barman, wiping his hands on a greasy apron. He was a great hairy man with an untrimmed red beard.

'I'll have a scotch and water,' said Crispin.

'Aye, and whit aboot yer daughter?'

'I'll have the same,' said Alison.

'My *friend* will have the same,' said Crispin, who wondered at the same time why barmen the length and breadth of the British Isles usually referred to his female companion as his daughter, no matter what age the lady was, not knowing his offensive manner always prompted the time-honoured insult.

They sat down at a rickety plastic table by the window with their drinks.

'This is fun,' said Crispin. 'I like these quaint old places. It's amazing when you look about places like this and realize that Britain still does have a peasantry.'

One of the small men turned from the bar and approached their table. He went straight up to Crispin who smiled at him weakly and then before Crispin or Alison could guess what the man was about to do, he whipped off his cap and butted Crispin on the forehead.

Crispin groaned and clutched his head.

'You assaulted him!' screamed Alison. 'I'll call the police.'

But the word *police* seemed to have an amazingly restorative effect on Crispin. 'I'm fine,' he said. 'Let's get out of this smelly place.'

When they got outside, Alison noticed he looked white and shaken and there was a lump beginning to form on his forehead.

'I'd best get you back,' said Alison. 'Are you sure you're all right? I mean, I could call the police.' Fern Bay was probably on Hamish's beat, thought Alison, and then remembered Hamish's cruelty of the previous evening.

'No, no, I'll be all right in a tick. That little bastard. Did you see the way he just put his cap back on and went back to his drink as if nothing had happened?'

'It's because you're English,' said Alison soothingly. 'They don't like the English and I don't suppose they like being called peasants either.'

Maggie was waiting for them when they got back. She was holding a pile of typed manuscript.

'I've made some changes,' she said nastily to Alison, 'so you better get in there and start typing.'

'Alison said you were writing a book. Are we all in it?' asked Peter Jenkins.

'Wait and see,' said Maggie with a husky laugh. The four men who were in the living room exchanged uneasy looks. Maggie rounded on Alison. 'Well, stop standing there like a drip and get to work!'

'I'd like a word with you in private, Maggie, now!' said Peter.

'Very well. Come outside.'

Alison went into the study, feeling a little glow of warmth. Peter was going to give Maggie a telling off about her harsh treatment of her. The study window overlooked the garden. Alison longed to hear what Peter was saying. She pushed open the window and listened hard.

Peter's well-modulated drawl reached her ears quite clearly.

'This advertising business of mine has been going through some hard times, Maggie,' she heard him say. 'But I've got some new top clients and the money will be coming through soon. If you could see your way to lending me a few thousand, I can pay you back at the end of six months and at a good rate of interest, too.'

'So you want my money without having to marry me to get it?' said Maggie.

'Oh, love, come here and give me a kiss. If I thought I had a hope in hell of getting you, I wouldn't have asked . . .'

Alison closed the window and sat down, feeling miserable. No one loved her, Hamish was fed up with her and Peter and Crispin were only making up to her because they thought she had an in with Maggie.

The study door opened and James Frame sidled in. 'I say . . .' he began tentatively.

'If you've come to ask me to put in a word with Maggie, forget it!' said Alison bitterly. 'She hates me and I hate her and I wish I were dead but I'd like to see her in her grave first!'

'Gosh, you are in a tizzy,' said James, smoothing down his patent leather hair with a nervous hand. 'I only came to ask you . . . well, don't you see, it's that damn book that's worrying me. Be a good chap and tell me if she's got me in it.'

Alison looked at him with loathing. She hated them all. 'You're all in it,' she said spitefully, 'and highly pornographic it is, too. Do be an angel and tell the rest, won't you? I'm sick of being pestered and I've got work to do.'

The study door opened again and this time Maggie walked in. She stopped short at the sight of James. If Alison had listened at the window a little bit longer, she would have heard Peter defending her. That and the fact that her niece had been out driving with Crispin had put Maggie in a towering rage. The sight of James bending over Alison was the last straw.

'When you've finished typing that book,' said Maggie to Alison, 'you can pack your things and leave.'

'But I've got nowhere to go,' said Alison weakly.

'Listen, Alison,' said Maggie, 'you're got your health and strength so I suggest you stop sponging off me and start working for a living. That whey face of yours makes me sick. I expect you to be out by the end of the week.'

'Could I have a word with you, beautiful?' oiled James.

Maggie went in for one of her lightning changes of mood. 'Of course,' she murmured seductively. 'Come up to my bedroom.'

Alison sat, numb with misery, but somewhere at the bottom of her misery was a tiny feeling of relief. The door opened again and she heard Steel Ironside's Liverpudlian accents. 'Well, that's that. She's taken that gaming club creep up to her room. He's probably getting his leg over right now.'

Alison sat, rigid and silent.

The pop singer began to pace up and down the room. He was wearing a black cotton shirt open to the waist, revealing a thick mat of grey

chest hair in which nestled a large gold medal-
lion. 'God, I could do with a bit of her money,'
he said. 'I know I've got a hit. But I need the
money for a backing group and then the hire
of a studio.'

Alison began to cry. She had been crying
such a lot lately that the tears came easily,
splashing on to the typewriter.

'Hey, what's up, luv?' The pop singer sat
down on a chair beside Alison and peered at
her through his half-moon glasses.

'Maggie's throwing me out at the end of the
w-week,' hiccupped Alison.

'Haven't you any place to go?'

Alison dumbly shook her head.

'Here. Give me a piece of paper. There's
these bods in a squat down in Liverpool who'll
take you in. Give them this note.'

'You're very kind,' said Alison when she
could, although she thought she would rather
die than move in with a lot of Liverpudlian
squatters who were probably all high on dope.

'Fact is, the four of us were talking about
you this morning. Maggie's gone on so much
about her bad heart, in the event of her dying
soon, we was saying it might be better for
one of us to marry you and then divvy up the
takings.'

'If Maggie died,' said Alison, 'I would take
the money, keep it, and throw you all out. I
hate Maggie and I hate you.'

But he merely laughed and patted her head.
'Maggie's turned out a right bitch,' he said.

'She's enough to turn the milk. When I think what a smasher she was, warm and beautiful. Right bloody cow she is now. Don't take it out on me. With any luck, she'll drop dead. I'll survive somehow.'

'I'm sorry if I was rotten to you,' said Alison, 'but you all seem so mercenary. Not one of you seems to like Maggie.'

'It's all very well to live in slums and eat baked beans when you're young,' said Steel, half to himself, 'but one day you wake up old and broke and the thought of going back and starting all over is scary. Know what I mean?'

'I'm going to have a cup of coffee,' said Alison, getting to her feet. 'Coming?'

'Sure. Lead the way.'

Mrs Todd was in the kitchen and looked anxiously at Alison's tearstained face. 'Whit's the matter, bairnie?' she said.

Alison told her of Maggie's throwing her out.

'Maybe she's worried about something,' said Mrs Todd. 'Mrs Baird's a fine decent woman and –'

'Decent!' Alison's laugh was shrill. 'I never told you, Mrs Todd, but she was and still is a tart. You should read that book of hers . . .'

'Don't be saying nasty things about herself,' said Mrs Todd soothingly.

'S'right, all the same,' said Steel, slouching around the kitchen with his hands thrust into the pockets of his jeans. 'Real old whore is our Maggie.'

'I will not be having that language in my kitchen!' Mrs Todd was quite pink with outrage. The pop singer grinned and strolled out.

'Don't worry your head at the moment,' said Mrs Todd. 'I have a wee bit cottage in the village and I can put you up there until you get on your feet.'

'Thank you,' said Alison weakly. But inside her head another prison door seemed to slam. She only half realized that she would probably accept Mrs Todd's invitation and therefore say goodbye to any hope of independence. 'I'd better get back to work,' said Alison, picking up the cup of coffee Mrs Todd had poured for her.

The bungalow had gone suddenly quiet. In her misery, she vaguely wondered where everyone was.

She sat down at the desk and forced herself to begin typing, trying to divorce her mind from the words. She heard a noisy chattering and clattering as they all met for lunch but could not bring herself to join them. She typed steadily on.

And then in the afternoon, Maggie came in. She sat down in a chair beside the desk.

'Look here, Alison,' she said in her new husky voice 'You mustn't take me too seriously these days. Fact is, my nerves are screaming and I take it out on you.'

Alison sat very still, her fingers resting on the keys.

'I don't know what's up with me,' Maggie went on. 'Half the time I seem to hate the world and I think if I see another bowl of salad, I'll puke.'

'You weren't very nice to me when you were fat either,' said Alison in a low voice.

'It's your own fault. There's something kickable about that cringing air of yours, sweetie. You can stay. I wish I'd never invited this lot. But I want to get married again and all men are much the same.'

'But why these four?' asked Alison, curious despite her distrust of Maggie's sudden friendliness.

'They are the ones who were actually in love with me . . . once,' said Maggie. 'I got a private detective on to them and found out they all need money. I don't rate my charms that high. Stuff Women's Lib. It's still rotten trying to get the maitre d' in a restaurant if you're a single woman. And when it comes to business, men only want to deal with men. Other women pity you if you're on your own. I like a man about the place, God knows why. Anyway, it's no use looking for romance. In a marriage it all comes down to the same thing in the end: "Why do you keep losing my socks?" But I've never settled down long enough with any man to find out what it's all about. The minute one of them got difficult, I'd give him his marching orders. Cheer up, sweetie, you're still in my will.'

'I'm not interested in your money,' said Alison untruthfully.

Maggie studied her for a moment and her face softened. 'I think you mean that. God! I'm a bitch. Try not to take any of my moods personally. So you'll stay?'

Alison looked up into Maggie's blue eyes and received the full force of that lady's considerable personality.

'Yes,' she said weakly.

'Good girl.' Maggie gave her a hug, the Maggie of old, the Maggie who had swept into the hospital, the warm, maternal Maggie.

For the rest of the day, Alison felt happier than she had since Maggie's return. Maggie's change of mood permeated the house. Tomorrow, thought Alison, I'll ask her about the car.

Peter Jenkins went out of his way to be particularly nice to Alison, and Maggie did not seem to mind.

Alison slept late and awoke to the sound of the garage doors being opened.

The car!

Maggie must be about to drive it.

All at once Alison felt she just had to ask her about that car.

She threw on a dressing gown and ran downstairs and out on to the drive. The engine was coughing and choking. Maggie did not seem to be able to start it. Alison walked forward and stood in front of the car just as

Maggie wrenched the key once more in the ignition.

One minute Alison saw Maggie's beautiful face quite clearly through the windscreen. The next, it had vanished behind a sheet of flame.

Chapter Five

O Death, where is thy sting-a-ling-a-ling
O Grave, thy victoree?
The bells of Hell go ting-a-ling-a-ling,
For you but not for me.
                    – British Army song

Alison had often had that very common night-mare where one opens one's mouth to scream and no sound comes out. But the scream that was wrenched from her filled the air with dreadful sound, rushing away to the high hills, sending a taunting far-off mockery of a scream echoing back.

Peter Jenkins came running out in his dress-ing gown and slippers to where Alison stood with scream after scream pouring from her contorted face. He ran to the blazing car, flap-ping his hands ineffectually.

Steel Ironside erupted on to the scene with the kitchen fire extinguisher which he directed at the blazing car. 'Help me, you faggot!', he shouted at Peter Jenkins. He ran to the car door and wrenched it open, cursing as he did so.

He grabbed Maggie and dragged her out on to the garage floor, beating at the flames on her clothes, panting and sobbing.

Mrs Todd drove up. Her face was as white as paper as she ran for the house. She seized the phone in the kitchen and dialled 999 and demanded the fire brigade, the ambulance, and the police.

Then she went out and struck the still-screaming Alison across the face. Alison hiccupped and then ran to Peter Jenkins who gathered her into his arms.

Mrs Todd then crouched down by Maggie. 'She's dead,' said Steel in a flat voice. 'Her clothes had just started to catch fire when I pulled her out. She must have had a heart attack. She killed herself. I've never known anyone to mangle a car the way she did.'

Crispin and James arrived on the scene, both in pyjamas.

While Peter Jenkins, still holding Alison, explained in a hushed voice what had happened, Steel said, half to himself, 'It'll take hours for anything to reach us in this wilderness.' The wind of Sutherland howled across the sudden hush but far away came the sound of a siren.

It came nearer, ever nearer, until the Lochdubh Volunteer Fire Brigade rolled into the drive. Close behind came Hamish Macbeth.

'Nothing for us to do now,' said the fire chief, taking off his helmet and revealing himself to be Mr Johnson, the hotel manager. He looked at the car. Smoke was still rising from the bonnet. The front of the car was burnt black.

'Don't touch anything,' said Hamish Macbeth sharply. 'A forensic team will have to look at that car.'

'No need for that,' said Crispin, marching up in all the glory of primrose-yellow silk pyjamas. 'We all know Maggie wrecked that car. Something's gone in the engine and it burst into flames and gave her a heart attack. She could have got clear if she hadn't had an attack. The doors weren't locked. You policemen always complicate matters.'

'Indeed? Then I'm going to complicate them further,' said Hamish quietly. 'The minute the ambulance has been and gone, I'll start taking statements.'

Hostile eyes looked at him. Even Alison, despite her distress, thought he was being over-officious.

Hamish went back to the Land Rover. He did not believe the car had just burst into flames through some fault. Dr Brodie had arrived and was examining the body. Hamish called Strathbane and reported a suspected murder.

When the ambulance rolled up, Hamish said in a flat voice, 'Leave the body where it is.' Everyone looked at him: Alison, Mrs Todd, the four guests, the fire brigade, the doctor, and the ambulance men.

'What's up with you, Hamish?' snapped Dr Brodie. 'It's a clear case of a heart attack. I know you've solved murders in the past, but don't let it go to your head, laddie.'

'I've reported a suspected murder attempt,' said Hamish. The silence that followed that statement almost hummed in the ears. Then Hamish said sharply, 'Who raised the bonnet of the car?'

'Och, we only lifted it up to make sure there was no flames left underneath,' said Mr Johnson crossly.

'You shouldnae hae touched anything,' said Hamish. 'Mrs Todd, I think if you take Miss Kerr and the guests into the house, I'll come with you and start taking statements. We'll need to wait until the team arrives from Strathbane.'

'I'll hae a word to say to your superiors,' raged Mrs Todd. 'You cannae see a straight-forward death when you come across it. When my man died, you was ferreting around my cupboards looking for poison.'

'Had you told me your husband drank to excess, I wouldnae hae had to bother,' pointed out Hamish. 'I was acting under orders from the procurator fiscal.' The late Mr Todd had choked to death on his vomit and poisoning had been suspected. It had indeed turned out to be poisoning, but alcohol poisoning. Mrs Todd always maintained her husband had died of a heart attack.

Mrs Todd went grimly into the house and began to make preparations for a breakfast-cum-lunch while the others shuffled silently into the sitting room. 'Is there a room I can use?' Hamish asked Alison.

'What? Oh, yes. The study. Through there.'

'Perhaps you would like to come through first, Miss Kerr. No, there is no need for you,' he said to Peter, who rose at the same time as Alison and showed every sign of accompanying her.

Hamish sat down at the desk in the study. Alison had stopped crying. She looked ill.

'Just tell me what you were doing this morning,' said Hamish.

'I heard the car start, or rather I heard the garage doors being opened,' said Alison in a shaky voice. 'She . . . Maggie . . . had been kind to me the day before, so I thought I would ask her if I could drive the car. I ran down and out and just as I got to her, the car burst into flames.'

'Was there any sort of bang? Any sort of explosion?'

Alison tried to concentrate. 'No,' she said at last. 'One minute I saw her face quite clearly through the windscreen, and then it had vanished and there was nothing but flame.' She showed every sign of being about to cry again.

'Now,' said Hamish quickly, 'let's get to the house guests. The tall one who came down that night to the police station with ye, that's Peter Jenkins. What do you know about him?'

'He's an advertising executive in his own company,' said Alison. 'He knew Maggie about twenty years ago, I think, or did he say eighteen? Anyway, he was in love with her and then he got her letter. You see, she wanted to get married and so she had chosen four of her old lovers. You don't seem surprised?'

'I'm surprised at her odd way of courting but not that she had a lot of lovers. Go on.'

'He told me she'd changed. He wasn't in love with her anymore although I heard . . .'

Alison bit her lip. She had been about to tell Hamish about overhearing Peter begging for money, but Peter had held Alison and comforted her and she felt she had to protect him.

'What were you about to say?' demanded Hamish sharply.

Alison looked mutinous. He sighed and said, 'I'll return to that. Tell me about the others.'

'The smallish man in the yellow pyjamas is Crispin Witherington. He owns a car salesroom in Finchley in North London. He took me out driving. He wanted me to put a good word in for him with Maggie.'

'Now why would he suggest that? You said yourself Maggie hated you.'

'He thought Maggie was fond of me to leave me everything in her will . . .' Alison looked at Hamish with dilated eyes.

'Don't be in a taking,' said Hamish quickly, frightened that Alison would start another scene. 'The fact the woman left you her money doesn't mean you killed her for it.'

'It's not that,' said Alison. 'How did he know? I mean, how did he know that Maggie had left me her money? And how did Steel Ironside know?'

'Maybe she told them.'

'She simply wrote to them all inviting them,' said Alison, 'and then she told them on the first night that whoever married her would get her money and that she had a weak heart.'

'But she didn't tell them she had left it to you?'

'Not that I know of. She may have said it in her letters. She told me that when she decided on one of them, she would change her will and cut me out. Maybe they overheard that. It's very easy to hear things in this house. Oh, Hamish, only yesterday she apologized for being so rude to me and she said she wouldn't cut me out of her will. Everyone will think I did it. But it *can't* be murder.'

'Maybe it isn't. Go on about Mr Witherington.'

'I don't know any more except that he was one of Maggie's old flames. She made a profession of it.'

'Getting money from men?'

'Yes.'

'All right. Now let's move to James Frame.'

'He runs a gambling club in London. He wanted me to put in a word with Maggie as well. He seems harmless enough. I didn't have much of a chance to speak to him.'

'And Steel Ironside?'

'He's a failed pop singer. He told me he needed money to get started again. He seems nice. Oh, Hamish, I've just remembered. I asked Maggie why she was sure that one of these four would want to marry her and she said she'd had a private detective to check up on them and they all need money.'

'Good. I'll have a look through her papers and see if I can find the name of the detective agency. Send in your friend, Peter.'

Alison was soon replaced by Peter Jenkins. Hamish looked at him curiously. But he seemed just the same as he had done when Hamish had first met him: a pleasant, if weak, man, slightly effeminate. He looked at Hamish with dislike. 'You're making a fuss over nothing,' said Peter, 'and causing a great deal of unnecessary distress. The sooner someone higher up arrives, the better. It's a clear case of accident.'

'So you say. Let's get down to business. Full name . . .?'

In his slow drawling voice, Peter outlined the bare facts. He had been in love with Maggie twenty years ago and had only really fallen out of love with her when he arrived and found her changed. She had invited him for two weeks and he had taken leave from his firm. He needed a holiday and so he had decided to stay.

And all the time he was talking, Hamish was thinking, He's been carrying the torch for years for a prostitute. He must be awfully

immature. I wonder how he manages to run a company.

'How did you manage to set up this company?' he asked when Peter fell silent.

'I had been working for Sandford and Jones,' said Peter, naming one of the biggest advertising agencies. 'I was thirty when a rich uncle died and left me quite a bit so I decided to go into business for myself. My firm is Jenkins Associates.'

'Doing well?'

'Very well. We've got the Barker Baby Food account, for example.'

'Barker was bought out by a Japanese company last year. Do they still retain your services?'

'Of course. Didn't I just say so?'

Hamish sat back and surveyed Peter in silence.

Peter stared at him and then suddenly shrugged and said boyishly, 'I shouldn't lie. A vice of advertising men. Fact is, I had this friend working with me right from the beginning and he recently quit and took that account with him. I hope the Japanese dump him.'

'And what were you doing last night and this morning?'

'I was asleep the whole time. I heard Alison scream and rushed out.'

'And did you hear any explosion, any loud bang?'

'No, nothing, but there could have been one before Alison woke me with her screams. It was an accident.'

'Very well, Mr Jenkins. That will be all for now. Send in Mr Witherington.'

Crispin Witherington was very jovial and hearty. Then he obviously decided that jollity was out of place and became pompous.

He outlined the facts about his relationship with Maggie, where he was during the night and morning – in bed – his business, and his home address in a way that led Hamish to believe he had had dealings with the police before. Then he launched into a diatribe about the pub in Fern Bay and the attack on him.

'Why didn't you report it?' asked Hamish.

'What's the point,' said Crispin rudely. 'You local yokels stick together.'

'Don't be cheeky,' said Hamish mildly. 'Did you want to marry Mrs Baird?'

'Hadn't made my mind up. I only came up for a giggle.'

'And yet you asked Miss Kerr for help?'

'That sneaky little drip would say anything. Look, if it is murder, you only have to look in that direction.'

'Are you saying you didn't ask Miss Kerr for help?'

'I can't remember every blasted word I've said.'

'I'll be getting back to you. I'll hae a word with Mr Frame next.'

James Frame sidled in, smoothing down his already smooth hair with a nervous hand. Without prompting and with many 'don't you knows' and 'I says', he launched into his tale of how he had been asleep the whole time.

He had almost perfected the silly-ass manner, thought Hamish, but the man's eyes behind a glaze of helpful and innocent goodwill were hard and watchful as if a smaller, meaner man were staring from behind thick glass. When he had met Maggie, he said, oh-so-long-ago, he had been doing a bit of this and that. Money in the family, don't you know. All the while, Hamish made mental notes. Lower middle class. Accent assumed. Probably was a small-time crook.

'I believe Mrs Baird was very expensive,' said Hamish.

'She wasn't a whore,' said James indignantly. 'We were very much in love. Of course, a chap helps out a bit with the rent and things like that, but a chap would do that for any girl.'

'What is the name of the gambling club where you work?'

'The Dinosaur in Half Moon Street. That's Mayfair.'

'Yes, I know where Half Moon Street is. Do you own The Dinosaur?'

'Well, not zactly. Run it for a chap.'

'And the chap's name?'

'Harry Pry.'

'Champagne Harry. Out of prison is he?'

James looked sulky.

Even Hamish had heard of Harry Fry. He was a con artist. His last fling had been to ingratiate himself into the graces of a colonel who was a close friend of the royal family and who lived in a grace and favour house in Windsor, that is a rent-free house given by the Crown. The colonel had gone to the Middle East to raise money for one of his favourite charities, Save the Donkeys, and had left Harry alone in his house. Harry had sold the house for a vast sum to an Arab and had been caught just as he was about to board a plane to Brazil at London airport.

His sentence had been surprisingly lenient. He had great charm and had used it to good effect in court. He had paid back all the money he had gained for the house. Harry was reputed to be worth millions. He tricked and conned only because it was the breath of life to him.

At last Hamish sent James off and Steel Ironside took his place.

'Real name?' asked Hamish.

'Victor Plummer,' said the pop singer in a sulky voice. But asked about his previous relationship with Maggie, he perked up and grew almost lyrical. He might have been describing a teenage romance: Maggie's arrival on the scene, their first meeting at a party where she had shown no interest in him, the long tours, the sleezy hotels and theatrical digs, the sudden fame, the just-as-sudden falling in love and the start of the affair with Maggie, the walks in the park, the dog they had bought, the plans they had made.

'And why did she leave you?' asked Hamish.

Steel's face darkened. 'Someone else came along,' he said in his flat, nasal twang.

'Another pop singer?'

'No, Sir Benjamin Silver, head of Metropolitan Foods.'

'The multimillionaire?'

'Yes.'

'I see.'

'I didn't at the time,' said Steel. 'That was the thing about Maggie. She went through a mint of my money but I never thought of it as paying her. I mean, she wasn't the kind you left the money on the bedside table for. I was in love and I thought she was. I thought she would come back to me.'

'Are you married?'

'Separated.'

'So how could you have married Mrs Baird?'

'I'd have got a divorce. Never got around to it before.'

What a weak bunch of men, thought Hamish. He took some more notes and then braced himself to interview Mrs Todd.

He took down Mrs Todd's account of her arrival on the scene of Maggie's death and then began to ask questions. Why had Mrs Todd not rushed to see if she could help instead of going straight to the house and dialling 999? What had led her to believe no one had yet dialled?

'I do not know,' she said primly. 'It all happened that quick. They're a useless bunch and wouldnae think o' doing anything sensible.'

'Very well. Where were you last night and this morning?'

'I was at a meeting of the Women's Rural Institute at the school hall, went tae my bed, and then collected some groceries in the village and drove up here.'

'Do you know where Mrs Baird meant to go?'

'I don't know. Herself usually didn't move till the afternoon. Let me tell you this, Mr Macbeth, you are making a lot of trouble over a mere accident. You are causing poor little Miss Kerr a lot o' strain.'

Hamish ignored that and ploughed patiently on with his questions.

In the sitting room, Alison sat on the sofa with Peter Jenkins beside her. His arm was around her shoulders.

'So much for that *helpful* copper of yours,' said Peter. 'I'll have his guts for giving us all this trouble.'

'He wasn't at all sympathetic,' sniffed Alison. 'Sitting there like the Gestapo. I don't know what's come over him.'

'Power, that's what. These local hick types love a chance to push their betters around.'

Alison leaned back and closed her eyes. She thought about her recent interview with Hamish. She and Hamish had been friends and yet he had asked her questions as if he had never known her. God! How she hated that study. She would have it turned into a breakfast room or a library. She hated the functional desk where she had typed so much filth.

She sat up a little, frowning.

'What's the matter?' asked Peter.

'The manuscript,' said Alison. 'Maggie's book. I don't remember seeing it on the desk. I'd better tell Hamish about it.'

'She was in there last night,' said Peter. 'She probably either took it to her room or put it in one of the drawers. But tell that dreary bobby if you like.'

The four guests had been looking forward to the arrival of Hamish Macbeth's superior, and when he did arrive, Detective Chief Inspector Blair from Strathbane did not let them down. It was, he said, a clear case of accident. There was no need to use a squad of policemen to comb the area for clues. The car would be towed away to Strathbane and examined there. He was sure the wiring would prove to be faulty. He was so delighted at putting Hamish down before an audience that he was even nice to Steel Ironside, despite the fact that he remembered clearly that one of the pop singer's hits in the early seventies had been 'Burn the Fuzz'. Mrs Todd served him coffee with cream and some of her scones. His two detectives, Jimmy Anderson and Harry

MacNab, stood respectfully behind his chair. Alison, who told him about Maggie's vicious treatment of the car, thought Blair a nice fatherly man. He was heavyset and spoke with a thick Glasgow accent and when not being nice to the company treated Hamish like a moron. And Hamish deserved it all, thought Alison fiercely. After all, Hamish was a Highlander and the Highlanders were another race entirely, sly and malicious and devious.

But as if remembering at last that he, too, was a policeman, Blair became mindful of his duties and told the four men to stay at the bungalow until the forensic report came through. In a quiet voice, Hamish told him of the missing manuscript and its contents. 'Hot stuff, hey?' said Blair with a salacious leer. 'I may as well hae a gander at it. Go and find it, Macbeth, and dae something useful fur a change.'

Hamish went off. He searched Maggie's desk and then moved quietly upstairs to her bedroom and went carefully through all the drawers. But there was no sign of the manuscript and no sign either of any report from a detective agency.

At last Blair left, and the shaken guests and Alison settled down to have lunch in the kitchen.

James looked out of the window and muttered something and then got to his feet and went over and stared out. 'Someone had better get on to Strathbane,' he said. 'That local bobby's making trouble.'

The others joined him at the window.

The rain had started to fall quite heavily, but Hamish Macbeth, accompanied by a large mongrel dog, was down on his hands and knees on the gravel in front of the garage, slowly going over every inch of ground.

'Oh, let him get on with it,' said Peter Jenkins impatiently. 'He's better out there than in here bothering us with a lot of questions.'

They all returned to the table but no one seemed to feel much like eating and at last with a clucking noise of impatience, Mrs Todd removed the plates of unfinished food.

Hamish, oblivious to the rain, slowly edged backwards over the gravel, his nose almost on the ground. Then he moved over to the narrow strip of grass that bordered the right-hand side of the drive. He worked his way along, backing towards the two gateposts.

And then at the bottom of one of the gateposts he found a blackened piece of metal. He looked at it thoughtfully and then fished in his pocket for tweezers and plastic bag and popped it in.

He worked his way forward again while Towser let out a little whimper of dismay and shook himself violently, sending out a spray of water over Hamish's back. Hamish was just about to give up his search when close by where the car had stood in the garage he found a tiny piece of charred material like felt.

He put that in the bag with the metal and then decided to go and see Ian Chisholm.

'Bad business up at the bungalow,' said Ian. 'Mind you, that car was a wreck. I hadnae seen it since I did the last repairs but it wisnae in very good shape then and that lassie, Alison, well, herself must hae driven it thousands o' miles. I suppose it just all blew.'

'Maybe,' shivered Hamish, steaming gently in front of the black cylindrical wood-burning stove in a corner of the garage. 'But just suppose, Ian, just suppose you wanted a car tae burst into flames, would this mean anything tae ye?' He extracted the piece of blackened metal and the little bit of cloth from the plastic bag, holding each item up by the tweezers.

Ian scratched his grey hair. 'My, my, ye're after another murder,' he said. 'Well, let me hae a think, but it'll cost ye.'

'Come on, Ian, I'm not asking a favour, I am asking ye to help the forces of law and order solve a murder.'

'A murder that Blair has decided is an accident?'

'Now how did you hear that?'

'Angus Burnside, him that did the garden for Mrs Baird from time tae time, him was up at the house for he heard the siren and went for a look-see. He was still there when Blair and two fellows come out and he hears Blair say, "I'll hae that Macbeth's balls fur trying to call an accident murder."'

'I forgot about Angus,' said Hamish. 'I'd better hae a wee word with him. Anyway, use your brain, Ian.'

'I hae a Renault same age as hers, over here,' said Ian. He went over to a corner of the garage where a battered Renault with a crushed side stood. He raised the bonnet and peered at the engine. Then he called Hamish over. 'Let's see that bit o' metal again,' said Ian. Hamish took it out with a pair of tweezers and held it up. 'Don't touch!' he warned.

'Aye, that's a spark plug,' said Ian. 'Look, it could just be done, Hamish, and here's how.'

'Now, if someone removed the high-tension lead from a spark plug, and stuck this lead on to another spark plug and laid it on top of the engine, immediately someone tried to start the engine, a spark would ignite the fumes which could be coming from, say, a petrol-soaked mat of felt resting on the engine, and, man, you'd get a bonny fire. But it still cannae be murder.'

'Why not?'

'Well, although the engine would burst into flames, herself would still hae time to open the door and get clear. She'd only get a fright.'

'And if that someone knew she had a bad heart?'

'Aye, man, well in that case you'd have a murder.'

Chapter Six

I am a conscientious man, when I throw
rocks at seabirds I leave no tern unstoned.
                                    – Ogden Nash

Now, thought Hamish Macbeth, if I phone
Blair as a good copper should, Blair will tell
me I'm talking rubbish and then slide along to
the super and put it in as his own idea. If I am
as unambitious as I keep telling Priscilla I am,
then why should I bother? But damn it, I *do*
bother.'

He went into the police station office and
pulled forward the typewriter and began to
type out a report. When it was finished, he
drove to the hotel, and despite Mr Johnson's
caustic remarks about mooching scroungers,
he ran off three copies of the report on the
hotel's photocopying machine. Then he
headed out towards Strathbane.

He found, as he drove into the town, that he
was experiencing a slight feeling of dread, as
if he would never escape again. He was glad
he had left Towser behind in Lochdubh. The

poor animal would probably think he was going back to the police kennels.

He drove to the police headquarters and left three of the reports plus the plastic bag with the spark plug and scrap of felt at the desk: one of the reports to go to Detective Chief Inspector Blair, one to Superintendent Peter Daviot, and one plus the bag to go to the forensic department. Then he went back out into the night.

He decided to celebrate with a drink before returning to Lochdubh. He cast his mind back over his busy day. He had not had anything to drink so he could indulge in a small glass of whisky without being in any danger of being over the limit.

Soon Hamish was standing at the bar of an unlovely pub called The Glen, which he had recently patrolled on his beat. It still reflected the Calvinistic days when drinking was a sin and the only point in going to a pub was to get drunk. There was a bar along the end of a small room. The floor was covered with brown linoleum. There were two tables, a battered upright piano, a juke box, and a fruit machine. The whole place smelled of beer, disinfectant, damp clothes, and unwashed bodies, the habitués of The Glen dating from the days when a bath was something you had before you went to see the doctor.

'Evening, Hamish,' said the barman. It had been a source of great irritation to PC Mary Graham that the locals on the beat all called

Hamish by his first name. 'Hivnae seen yiz for a long while.'

'I'm back in Lochdubh,' said Hamish. 'I'll hae a dram.'

'This one's on the hoose,' said the barman. 'Ye're sore missed, Hamish. That blonde scunner's aye poking her nose in here, looking for trouble.'

Correctly identifying the 'blonde scunner' as PC Graham, Hamish thanked him and then turned and looked around the busy bar. Several of the locals called greetings to him and he nodded cheerfully back. The customers were not working class, rather they were underclass, the denizens of the dole world who lived from one drink to the next. The juke box fell silent. A local who rejoiced in the nickname of Smelly MacCrystal lumbered to the piano. It was rumoured he had once been a concert pianist, but Hamish took that with a pinch of salt. All the habitués of The Glen claimed to have been something important at one time, from professors of English literature to jet pilots. But when only half drunk as he was that evening, Smelly could play well and he played all the old and favourite Scottish songs.

'Come on, Hamish,' shouted someone. 'Gie us a song.'

Hamish turned red with embarrassment. He had drunk far too much on the evening of that wonderful day when he was told he could go back home and he had celebrated in The Glen by entertaining the surprised locals to a concert. He shook his head but found himself being propelled towards the piano. He shrugged and gave in.

PC Mary Graham quietly pushed open the door of the pub, hoping, as usual, to catch someone breaking the law. She stood there amazed.

Hamish Macbeth was standing by the piano, his fiery hair gleaming in the harsh neon lights of the pub. He was singing 'My Love Is Like a Red, Red Rose'. Hamish was blessed with a good voice, that kind of voice which is often affectionately described as an Irish parlour tenor. But Mary noticed only that Hamish Macbeth was leaning on the piano, singing, and surrounded by a group of dirty drunks, and he was not in uniform.

She turned and sprinted for police headquarters. As she arrived, panting and breathless, Superintendent Peter Daviot was just coming down the stairs. Now Mary should have reported to the desk sergeant who would have taken the matter higher, but she was too desperate to get Hamish into trouble to bother about the niceties of police procedure. Daviot had been looking for Blair without success. He had Hamish's report in his briefcase. He had phoned the forensic department to learn they had not started to examine the car because Blair had told them the matter was not urgent.

He listened in amazement to Mary's story. One of his officers was howling drunk in one of Strathbane's sleeziest pubs.

'We'll use my car,' said Daviot. He was always worried about the police force's public image. He prayed one of the local reporters would not decide to visit the pub before he got there, the super being rather naive about the press and not knowing that if the papers wrote stories about every roistering copper, there would be little room on their pages for anything else.

He entered the pub just as Hamish was entertaining the company with a rendering of 'The Rowan Tree'. Daviot stopped short, listening to the mellow voice soaring in the well-known sentimental ballad. Several of the drunks were crying.

Hamish finished his song to noisy applause and shook his head when they demanded more. Then he saw the super and walked forward with a smile which quickly faded as he saw PC Graham's avid face behind the super's shoulder.

'Evening, sir,' said Hamish mildly. 'Did you get my report?'

'Yes, thank you,' said Daviot. 'It should have gone to Blair, you know.'

'I sent him a copy as well,' said Hamish. 'How did you know I was here?'

'PC Graham was most concerned about your behaviour. She said you were drunk.'

'I wonder why,' said Hamish pleasantly.

'I suppose because you are not in uniform and singing in a low pub.'

'This pub,' said Hamish firmly, 'was on my beat. You are very concerned with police image, sir, and I think you will agree that if you get along with the local community, then people are more likely to come to you in time of need.'

'Just so,' said the super. 'Just what I always say.'

'You will also agree that it iss verra important to get the facts right before troubling anyone. PC Graham should hae asked me a few questions. That way, she would hae found there iss no reason for me to wear uniform when off duty and that I wass not drunk.'

'You mean, she did not speak to you?'

'Not a word.'

Daviot swung round. 'Get back to your beat, Officer,' he said sternly to PC Graham, 'and then come and see me tomorrow.'

'Aye, that's right,' said one of the locals, peering over the super's arm. 'Tell Typhoid Mary to get the hell oot.'

PC Graham threw Hamish a venomous look before she left.

'Come out to the car, Hamish,' said the super. 'I can't talk in here.'

Hamish waved goodbye and followed Daviot out.

In the car, Daviot opened his briefcase and took out Hamish's report. 'You say here that

Mrs Baird had employed a private detective agency to find out about these men?'

'Yes,' replied Hamish, 'but I couldnae find any sign of it, nor of that book she said she was writing.'

'And what did Blair say to that?'

'He didnae seem interested,' said Hamish, wondering at the same time why sinking the knife in Blair's fat back should make him feel so mean.

'Very well. Go back to Lochdubh and leave the matter with me. It is entirely your own fault, Hamish, that you are not in charge of this case. You have avoided promotion deliberately. I am not complaining. Good village policemen are hard to find. On the other hand, I think it is time you took a good look at yourself. You should be thinking of marriage, for example.'

'I always wonder why detectives get married,' said Hamish. 'I mean, they're hardly ever home and the only friends they have outside the force are villains.'

'A good, sensible wife would make allowances. It's time you settled down. I know my wife got some nonsense into her head that you might marry Priscilla Halburton-Smythe, but I said to her you would be better off with some strong village girl to look after you and iron your shirts.'

'I am a dab hand wi' the iron myself,' said Hamish defensively.

'Well, you'll just need to go back to your regular duties and assist the detectives when and where they need you. You are a sore disappointment to me, Macbeth.'

And by that loss of his first name, Hamish knew the super was indeed angry with him.

But Daviot had given him a lot to think about. Blair would be back in Lochdubh on the morrow, throwing his weight around, and making life hell for everyone in general and Hamish Macbeth in particular. But to join the detectives, to live in Strathbane, thought Hamish as he drove slowly along the waterfront at Lochdubh. Would no one ever understand the happiness and contentment of the truly unambitious man?

Priscilla certainly did not. And there, as if his thoughts had conjured her up, standing outside the police station under the blue lamp, was Priscilla.

He jumped down from the car. 'When did you get back?'

'Today,' said Priscilla. 'Any chance of a cup of tea?'

Hamish led the way into the kitchen. He suddenly remembered that once when she had been in love with a yuppie called John Harrington, Priscilla had been a whole week in Lochdubh before she had thought to call on him.

John Harrington had been arrested for insider trading. Did Priscilla visit him in prison?

'See anything of that Harrington fellow?' he asked after he had made a pot of tea and they were sitting at the kitchen table.

'No, I can't. He was out on bail and he skipped the country.'

'There was nothing about it in the papers,' said Hamish.

'It was in the English editions. They probably didn't bother in Scotland.'

The bell went at the front of the station. 'Aren't you going to answer it?' asked Priscilla.

Hamish shook his head. 'It'll be the press. Let them go and bother Alison. So you're up for the summer. How are things at home?'

'Not very good. Daddy's blood pressure is dangerously high. Brodie says he's got to go on a diet, but Daddy says that's a lot of rubbish. You can't tell him anything. Something's worrying him badly. Mummy says he won't talk about it and just snaps that there's nothing up.'

'You look tired,' said Hamish, studying her.

The beautiful oval of her face looked as flawless as ever, but her mouth drooped at the corners and her eyes were weary and sad.

Priscilla shrugged. 'It wasn't a very good homecoming, which is why I am here. I felt in need of a friend. What's all this about Maggie Baird dying? Everyone thinks you a fool for saying it was murder. Tell me about it.'

So Hamish did, ending up with, 'Of course, it can't really be classified as murder since she died of a heart attack, so whenever we find out who rigged the car, he or she will be charged with culpable homicide, but everyone knew about her weak heart, so to my mind, it's murder.'

'And the obvious suspect is Alison.'

'Yes, it seems as if she inherits the lot. Money's usually the root of all murders, or passion, but the guests seem a weak, mercenary lot. Maggie told them she would give her money to the one she married and that she didn't expect to live long. Mind you, in that case, why didn't whoever wait till she changed her will? But I can't see Alison doing it.'

'Why not?'

'That one would dream about killing Maggie, but never actually do it. Or if by any remote chance she did, she would use poison. It's more of a man's murder. Crispin Witherington would know all about car engines. I'll find out about the others.'

The kitchen door opened and Alison Kerr walked in. 'Oh!' she said, looking at Priscilla in dismay. Priscilla half rose to leave, saw the look in Hamish's eye, and sat down again, putting an affectionate hand on Hamish's arm.

'Hamish!' said Alison, taking a chair on the other side of Hamish and gazing into his eyes. 'You have to do something. The press keep badgering me. They ring the bell and shout through the letterbox. What am I to do?'

'You get Mrs Todd to move into one of the spare bedrooms,' said Hamish wearily, 'and you get her to answer the door, and before you do that, you shut the gates to the house and don't open them unless you want to drive out.'

'But you have to come up and tell these reporters they are trespassing!'

'I cannae do a thing. There are no laws of trespass in Scotland. You've got four men in the house. Can't one of them cope?'

'Peter's been marvellous. He brought me down here. He's waiting outside. He knew the press would be coming so he parked his car outside, a little down the main road. So we crept out through the garden when the press weren't looking.'

'Did ye no' think of just walking through them and saying "No comment"? Obviously not. Get Mrs Todd. She'll handle them.'

'But I can't pay her to stay all night!'

'You phone the solicitors in the morning,' said Hamish patiently, 'and make sure you inherit. If you do, you ask them for what money you need. You could even put a down payment on a car.'

'A car! Oh, Hamish, you are clever,' said Alison, throwing her arms around him, all her anger at his previous cruelty forgotten.

'Yes, yes,' said Hamish testily, unwinding her arms from about his neck. 'I would appreciate it, Alison, if you would phone me next time you want to come here. As you can see, I am entertaining company.'

Alison blushed. Priscilla gave her a cool look

and said, 'Your friend must be wondering what's keeping you.'

'I'm going,' said Alison crossly. 'You don't *own* Hamish, you know.'

'My, my. Isn't money the wonderful thing,' said Hamish as Alison went out, slamming the door behind her. 'The worm's beginning to turn.'

'I don't like that girl one bit,' said Priscilla.

'Och, she's all right. She'll soon be married to another car.'

Alison tried to remind herself on the road home that she should be grieving for Maggie, but she could not feel particularly sad. How much had Maggie left? Thousands! And a car! A darling little car, all her very own.

'We'll look through her papers as soon as we get back,' said Peter with a smile. 'I know what you're thinking about. You want a car of your own.'

'Oh, Peter, you're sometimes so *perceptive*, you scare me,' breathed Alison.

Alison had not searched for the will before, feeling it would be just too vulgar and insensitive. But she and Peter went straight to the study as soon as they got in and began to search through the desk. Alison was beginning to despair when Peter found it in the very front of the top drawer where it suddenly seemed to materialize in that irritating way that things do when you want them desperately – as if the household imps had got tired of the game of hide and seek and decided to

let you find whatever it was you were looking for.

Alison opened it up. Her own name
seemed to leap up at her and then she read
on, frowning.

'What is it?' asked Peter. 'Hasn't she left you
anything?'

'Yes, but this is a new will. This is a copy.
She must have stopped off in Inverness on her
road home and made out a new one. Listen!
She says that if I die, the money and the pro-
ceeds from this house and her place in London
are to be divided equally among the four of
you, "the only men who ever really loved me",
that's what she says.'

Peter looked at her thoughtfully. 'Then
you'd better just hope that one of us isn't the
murderer,' he said.

Alison did what Hamish had suggested. The
lawyers said their Mr Brady was on his way to
see her and she could make any arrangements
with him. But, yes, they would most certainly
advance her any money she wanted.

Mr Brady arrived and read out the contents
of the will to a stunned audience. For Maggie
had been worth over a million pounds in
investments and property. 'No wonder,' said
Peter dryly, when the lawyer had left, 'that
they were so keen to lend you money.'

Mrs Todd agreed to live in. She demanded
three hundred pounds a week. Alison blinked

slightly at that but readily agreed to pay her. The terror of the press receded. Mrs Todd gave them all a piece of her mind and then firmly locked the main gates in their faces.

And while all this was going on, Hamish was dealing with a new superior. Blair had been taken off the case, although detectives MacNab and Anderson had been left on it. This detective chief inspector was called Ian Donati. His parents had come from Italy and settled in the Highlands. He was thin and sallow with clever black eyes and a lilting Highland voice. A Highland Italian, thought Hamish, thank God, having all the average Scotsman's respect for Italians.

Donati produced Hamish's report and questioned him closely. 'As you seem to have a record for solving murders, I think it would be better if you accompanied us to Baird's house and sit in while we interview everyone all over again,' said Donati. 'Forensic men were working all night on that car to come up with the same results as your local mechanic.' His manner was polite and impersonal.

Before they went into the bungalow, Anderson drew Hamish aside. 'Why did ye land poor auld Blair in the shit?' he asked. 'Blair's a good steady worker.'

'I thought you didnae like the auld scunner!' exclaimed Hamish.

'I'd rather hae him than Donati.'

Hamish grinned. 'Your common nose has

been put out o' joint. Donati's too classy for ye. No swearin', no slacking off, no boozing.'

'Well, he shouldnae give himself airs. His folks own a restaurant in Strathbane.'

'And your dad spent most of his life on the dole. You're an awfy snob, Anderson. That man's a breath o' fresh air to me. Come on.'

The guests and Alison and Mrs Todd did not like Donati. They found his quiet, dry manner and probing questions terrifying. Hamish watched and listened. Without quite saying it, Donati seemed to lay the cold facts out before the four guests: all were reported to be in need of money and were prepared to marry a woman that none of them had professed to like anymore. They all secretly blamed Alison for having dished the dirt on them to the police, not knowing it was Mrs Todd who had told the police in no uncertain terms that she had overheard each of the men saying that Maggie had changed a lot and all for the worse.

The four men then gave their fingerprints and signed their statements and were told they could leave any time they wanted provided they let the police know where they could be contacted. But all said they had taken leave from work and would stay. It was obvious to Hamish that Alison was to be the new target for their affections and perhaps Peter Jenkins had been clever at getting in first.

But Peter Jenkins thought that Alison might be capable of falling for, say, the pop singer and shrewdly thought that Alison clung to him because, until the reading of the will, he had been the only one to be particularly nice to her.

He was therefore relieved when Alison the next day asked him shyly if he would drive her down to the solicitors so that she could pick up a cheque from them. He readily agreed. Alison, desperate to buy a new car right away, did not even want to wait until the cheque cleared so Peter said he would put a down payment on a car for her and she could pay him as soon as she got the money. Alison spent a happy afternoon at a showroom out on Inverness's industrial estate looking at and trying out cars. To Peter's surprise, she fell in love with a bright red mini, the cheapest new car in the showroom. Made bold by Alison's timidity, he got the salesman to phone the solicitors and found to his relief that the showroom would accept Alison's cheque right away and cash it as soon as the lawyer's cheque cleared, for Peter knew he had very little left in his personal account.

That evening, it was Alison who was the centre of attention and she blossomed under it, convincing herself that her personal charms were the reason for all this sudden adoration.

And while they all fussed over Alison and paid her compliments, Donati was sitting with Hamish Macbeth in the Lochdubh police station. An efficient man, he had phoned Scotland Yard when he had first been put on the case, directly after Daviot returned from the pub after speaking to Hamish. He had asked Scotland Yard to phone all the private detective agencies in London. Scotland Yard had quickly found the right one and had faxed the agency's report to Strathbane.

'And here it is,' said Donati, still with that precise, dry manner. 'I'll run through it for you. Crispin Witherington is in bad trouble. Financially, I mean. He's been in trouble in the past. He was at the centre of an investigation into stolen cars a good time ago. He was making money hand over fist. Although nothing could be proved against him, it's my guess he went straight and, not being a good car salesman or a good manager, proceeded to lose money.

'James Frame is another steady character. From research into Maggie Baird's background, it seems she often moved about that half-world of the west end of London frequented by rich criminals, drinking with the Kray brothers, that sort of thing. Oh, he knows cars. He worked, get this, at one time for Witherington. Nothing ever pinned on him. That gambling club's been raided several times for drugs but nothing ever found.

'Peter Jenkins. Good family. Educated Westminster and Christchurch, Oxford. Not a good degree. Fourth in history. Did what ex-public school boys with iffy degrees in history do – joined an advertising agency as a copy writer. Worked up to the management side. Got inheritance. Started his own firm. Did well for a bit, mainly owing to brilliant partner who recently pulled out and went into separate business and took some of the best accounts with him. Needs money or firm will fold. No money left in the family. Only child, parents dead, rich uncle was the last hope.

'Steel Ironside, née Victor Plummer, comes from a village in the Cotswolds, must have adopted that accent. Sprang to fame in the late sixties during the drug culture and anti-establishment years. Was quite good-looking in a pretty, unisex sort of way, you'd never think it now to look at all that grey hair. Back in prominence in the seventies with protest songs. His hit, "We'll Change the World", is still sung at demonstrations but hardly by the type of people who'll pay any royalties. He wrote it. Married to some noisy slag in Liverpool. Two kids. Never sends them any money. Into drugs but who wasn't in that sort of world, nothing serious. Done a few times for carrying hash through London airport but always for himself. Never pushed or supplied. What a right lot of lulus our Maggie Baird picked.'

'Who else would fall in love with a prostitute?' said Hamish primly.

Donati looked at Hamish in surprise, and then bent his head quickly to hide a smile. 'Aye, maybe you're right,' he said. 'But the only one with a motive is Alison Kerr.'

146

Hamish clasped his hands behind his head and stared at the ceiling. 'I believe they all were in love with her at one time. She wasnae, I gather from Alison who was typing those memoirs which have mysteriously disappeared, the kind to just demand money for services rendered. It was all done under the guise of love. You know, clothes, jewels, payment disguised as presents. They're all weak men with king-sized egos. Maybe one of them nursed a lifelong grudge and wanted to get back at her. She'd developed a real bitchy manner. Could have tipped one of them over the edge. One of them could have known about the will, the new one Brady told us about. Och, but he would have to get rid of Alison.'

'Exactly. I think we'd better warn her, don't you?'

Alison was getting ready for bed when Mrs Todd knocked at the bedroom door to say 'thae polis' were back again. Alison opened the door. 'Do I have to see them?' she asked weakly. She was wearing one of Maggie's white satin nightdresses with a white satin negligee trimmed with maribou. Mrs Todd looked shocked. 'I'm surprised at you, lassie. Wearing a dead woman's clothes.'

'These were new,' said Alison defiantly. 'She'd never even taken them out of the box.'

'Well, you are not seeing the polis until you make yourself look decent,' said Mrs Todd, folding her arms across her aproned bosom.

Alison wanted to scream that she was mistress of the house and would wear what she liked, but she sulkily went back into the bedroom and soon reappeared in one of her old skirts and a sweater.

'Now, that looks like my wee lassie again,' said Mrs Todd. 'Come along and I'll stay with ye. It's that Macbeth that gets my back up. Too young for the National Service. He should hae been drafted as a young man. A stint in the army would hae knocked some o' the laziness oot o' him. I remember during the war when I was in the army . . .' But Alison closed her ears. She was tired of Mrs Todd's lectures. I'm fed up with her, thought Alison mutinously as she followed Mrs Todd down the stairs, but how can I get rid of her? I know. I'll sell this place and get away from her that way.

The new millionairess walked into the sitting room and both policemen rose at her entrance.

'You may leave us,' said Donati to the housekeeper.

'No, I'll stay right here,' said Mrs Todd.

'Do as you are told, woman!' snapped Donati.

'I'll be in the kitchen, Alison, if you want me,' said Mrs Todd, and Alison thought, She'll need to start calling me 'Miss Kerr'.

Donati said, 'We have established that Mrs Baird died because someone deliberately tampered with her car. It was culpable homicide!'

Alison let out a whimpering sound. Her eyes sought those of Hamish Macbeth. Hamish stood like the epitome of the bone-headed police officer, hands behind his back, eyes on the middle distance.

'If you did not have any hand in this attempt, then we fear your life may be in danger,' said Donati in that emotionless voice of his.

'Me! Why?'

'Because the four men here stand to benefit from your death. Unless, of course, the criminal is lucky enough to get you to marry him.'

Alison began to cry. Hamish reflected he had never known anyone in his life before who could cry as much as Alison Kerr.

Donati remained unmoved. 'A policeman will be on constant guard at the house. Tell him if you notice anything suspicious.'

Alison scrubbed her eyes. 'Can I have Hamish?' she pleaded.

'No, I need Macbeth on this case and he has his village duties as well. A policeman from Strathbane will be assigned to you. Now, I am sorry to keep you further but you must tell me more about that book you were typing. Did she mention any of the four men in it?'

Alison shook her head. Hamish, glancing at her, noticed a sudden flash of alarm in

Alison's eyes and wondered what she had just remembered.

'Well, I must ask you for the names of some of the men in the book. Also, did Mrs Baird have any special friend in her heyday, I mean around about the time these four men here would have been on the scene?'

While Alison talked, Hamish found himself beginning to feel useless. Donati was asking all the questions that he, Hamish, would normally have asked behind Blair's fat back. It was very hard to feel clever and superior with Donati around. And Blair's hatred and jealousy of him, Hamish reflected, was a compliment in a way. Donati treated him as an intelligent policeman on the beat should be treated, nothing more. I'm jealous, thought Hamish ruefully.

When they had left, Alison threw herself into Mrs Todd's sturdy arms and sobbed her heart out. 'Now, then,' said Mrs Todd, 'you come upstairs and I'll tuck you into bed. There, there. You poor thing. Men!'

All Alison's thoughts of asserting herself and getting rid of Mrs Todd disappeared. It was lovely to be mothered.

But as soon as Mrs Todd had switched out the light and left, Alison began to tremble. Which one of them would kill her for the money? Money was so important. She couldn't sleep. The wind sighed through the trees outside, a mourning sound. She shivered despite the centrally heated warmth of the room.

And then she heard a soft sound outside her door. She switched on the bedside light. The door handle began to turn. Alison opened her mouth to scream but the door opened quickly and revealed Peter Jenkins. 'What do you want?' asked Alison harshly.

He came and sat on the edge of the bed and looked down at her. 'I couldn't sleep,' he said. 'That detective made me feel like a criminal.' Peter was wearing a paisley silk dressing gown over his pyjamas and his hair was tousled. Alison found she could not feel afraid of him.

'I'm awfully scared,' she said. 'I can't sleep either.'

He took her hand in his. 'I'll sit with you for a bit.'

'Thank you,' said Alison shyly.

They fell silent, looking at each other. Then Peter slowly bent his head and kissed Alison gently on the mouth. She wrapped her arms around him and the next thing he was lying on the bed and a few kisses later, in the bed, and a few more and they had both managed to divest themselves of their nightwear with that strange agility of people who are determined to make love.

Their lovemaking was brief but satisfactory to both. Heaven, thought Alison just before she drifted off to sleep in Peter's arms, almost as good as driving.

Chapter Seven

Madam, I may not call you; mistress, I am
ashamed to call you; and so I know not what
to call you; but howsoever, I thank you.
                              – Queen Elizabeth I

Hamish realized on the following day that he
was letting his admiration for Donati stop him
from thinking clearly about the case. In the
past, he had relied on gossip and his own intu-
ition. He decided to follow his nose and go out
to the bungalow and see what he could see.

He parked his police Land Rover out on the
road. The air was clammy and still and the sea
was silent. The midges, those stinging Scottish
mosquitoes, were out in force, and he auto-
matically felt in his pocket for the stick of
repellent he always kept handy.

He walked quietly up to the kitchen door
and then paused as he heard the animated
sounds of conversation from within. He
walked to the window and cautiously peered
in. Mrs Todd and PC Mary Graham were

seated at the kitchen table, talking nineteen to the dozen.

He swore under his breath. He should have guessed that Strathbane would send a police-woman rather than a policeman to guard Alison.

He returned to his car and drove back down the road a little to one of those red telephone boxes you find in the isolated parts of the Highlands. This one was perched precariously on the edge of a cliff. He phoned the bunga-low and, disguising his voice, asked for Alison. 'Who is speaking?' demanded Mrs Todd sharply.

'Ian Chisholm,' said Hamish, and then waited.

When Alison answered the phone, he said quickly, 'It's Hamish. I'm at the phone box down the road. Can you come down and meet me?'

'I can't, Hamish,' said Alison airily. 'I'm busy right now.'

'It's very important,' said Hamish. 'It won't take long. And don't tell anyone where you're going.'

'All right,' said Alison and put down the receiver.

About ten minutes later, Hamish saw the little red mini, Alison's new pride and joy, nosing its way down the cliff road.

He waited until she had parked and then climbed into the passenger seat beside her.

'What's PC Graham doing inside the house?' asked Hamish. 'She's supposed to be on guard outside.'

'Well, she did ask for a cup of tea when she arrived but Mrs Todd told her she was supposed to be on duty at the gate. The policewoman went off and started marching up and down like a sentry on duty. Mrs Todd was fussing about the kitchen. She seemed edgy. She kept looking out of the window at ... Mary, is it? Then she said, "Come to think of it, I'd feel safer with her in here," and called her in and in about a few minutes time, they seemed to be the best of friends.'

'And why was that, do you think?'

'If you must know, Mrs Todd opened the conversation by saying she was glad it was a sensible policewoman and not that idiot, Macbeth, and Mary said you were a layabout and they fell to tearing you to bits. What did you want to see me about?'

'It's about that book. When Donati asked you if there was anything about the four men in that book, you said no, but you looked startled.'

'I'd just remembered something,' said Alison. 'I didn't want to tell Donati, because I felt like a spiteful fool. You see, I let them all think they were in it.'

'Oh, my! Now about the people you remembered in the book, you said Maggie had had one friend but you couldn't quite remember the name. You said it was Glenys something.'

155

'It's funny. I remembered during the night.' Alison blushed furiously. Hamish's eyes sharpened. Alison was wearing a soft green silk blouse tucked into one of her old skirts but with a broad green leather belt with a gold clasp at her waist. She was also wearing sheer tights and high heels. She had put on eye make-up and lipstick and Hamish couldn't flatter himself all this effort was for him. So Peter Jenkins managed to score, he thought privately.

'I just remembered all at once,' said Alison. 'It was Glenys Evans.'

'And where did she live?'

Alison shook her head.

'Anyway, I might be able to find her. Now the sooner this murderer, or would-be murderer, is caught, the better for you, Alison. I am sure all these men are rushing around you hoping to marry your fortune.'

'Some of them may just like me,' said Alison sharply.

'Aye, but you could talk to them and find out if any of them bore a grudge against Maggie.' For the first time Hamish turned the full force of his charm on Alison. 'It would be our secret.'

'Oh, yes,' said Alison, forgetting Peter for one glorious moment.

Hamish phoned Donati and gave him Glenys's name. But later on, his Highland curiosity got the better of him: He had an urge to talk to this woman himself. He went

156

straight down to the post office and demanded the London telephone books. There seemed to be a great number of Evanses. He slid his thumb down the list and then stopped in surprise. For there it was in clear type, Glenys Evans, Harold Mews, London W.1.

He went back to the police station and put through a call. An autocratic voice answered the telephone and identified itself as Glenys Evans.

'It is Hamish Macbeth from Lochdubh police in Sutherland,' began Hamish.

'Then you can stop right there,' said Glenys. 'I've already had some pig of a detective around here this morning with a most offensive manner.'

Of course, thought Hamish quickly, Donati would telephone the Yard and they would have a man on the job first thing.

'I'm very sorry a lady like yourself had such a nasty experience,' said Hamish. 'But you see, I hae a personal interest in the matter. I wass very fond o' Mrs Baird and I would like to get my hands on the villain who tried to murder her.'

'What! That clodhopper said she'd died of a heart attack.'

'A heart attack induced by someone rigging up her car so that it burst into flames when she turned the key in the ignition. She had four guests at the house, Crispin Witherington, James Frame, Peter Jenkins, and Steel Ironside at the time, and her niece, Alison.'

'I didn't know she had any relatives.' There was a long silence. 'All right,' said Glenys at last. 'If you come down here, I'll see what I can do to help.'

'I don't know if that is possible,' said Hamish cautiously.

'In that case, forget it.'

'I'll come,' said Hamish quickly. 'I'll get the sleeper down tonight and be with you in the morning.'

She gave him directions to her address and rang off.

If Blair had been on the case, thought Hamish, then he would just have disappeared off to London without saying anything. But Donati was a different matter.

Donati was staying at the Lochdubh Hotel. Hamish made his way there.

The detective listened to him in silence and then said colourlessly, 'You stepped out of line. It is certainly unfortunate the Yard sent along someone tactless who put her back up. Do not take such actions again without my permission, do you understand?'

'Yes.'

'Yes, what?'

'Yes, sir.' Hamish looked down at Donati, who was sitting in an armchair in the hotel lounge, with a tinge of surprise. 'Now I suppose you'd better go. We must put personalities aside and if this woman can give you anything useful, it will be worth your fare. You may go.'

And Hamish left. Blair never would have given him permission to go. Blair would have practically foamed at the mouth.

So why was it that he suddenly missed Blair?

Alison set about helping Hamish Macbeth. She felt she had everything in the world she had ever wanted except security. While the criminal remained at large, there was no peace, and every evening shadow held menace and every footstep on the stairs was that of an assailant. Unlike most bungalows, this one had most of the bedrooms on an upper floor with dormer windows. Peter Jenkins, Mrs Todd, and James Frame slept on the same floor as Alison, with Steel Ironside and Crispin Witherington in bedrooms off one of the two corridors that ran off the large sitting room. The dining room which adjoined the sitting room was little-used since Maggie's death, the guests preferring to eat their meals in the more cheerful kitchen. Another incentive to help was that despite her blossoming love for Peter Jenkins, Alison felt restless and wanted something to do to occupy her time. The efficient Mrs Todd had made all the arrangements for Maggie's funeral and Alison had weakly left it all to her.

Alison had replied to PC Graham's questions about where she had been that morning by saying evasively that she had felt upset and so had gone for a little drive. Mary told her sharply not to leave the house again without saying where she was going, leaving Alison feeling more like the hired help than the lady of the house. Mrs Todd added her own admonitions. Alison resented Mrs Todd all over again and kept away from her as much as possible, unfairly blaming her for Mary's high and mighty manner.

Alison took pencil and paper into the dining room to start making notes on what she already had gleaned about the men's relationships with Maggie. There was a better chance of being undisturbed in the dining room than in the study.

But no sooner had she started than Steel walked in.

'Feel like getting out of this place and going somewhere?' he asked.

Alison looked at him and thought he might still be quite presentable if he shaved and wore ordinary clothes. His shirts were always open to the waist showing that repulsive mat of hair.

'Where did you think of going?' she asked.

'Up the hill at the back. Get some fresh air.'

'All right,' said Alison.

To PC Graham's sharp question, Alison told the policewoman where they were going.

The couple walked past the garage and through a little gate in the garden fence and up a winding path that led to the top of a heathery hill behind the house. A stiff breeze had sprung up blowing warm air in from the Gulf Stream. They paused at the top of the hill and

160

looked at the view. Great clouds were rolling in from the Atlantic and down below, the restless sea was green with flying black shadows as the clouds passed overhead.

'Can you lend me any money?' asked Steel abruptly.

'I'll need to consult my lawyers. I don't have the money yet.'

'They'll advance it to you if you ask,' said Steel crossly. 'You've already got enough for that car of yours.'

'Well, it is *my* money now.'

'Look,' wheedled Steel, 'I've got this great song. I need money to launch it. I could pay you back with interest.'

'Let me think about it,' said Alison. 'Isn't the view pretty?'

'Bugger the view,' he said morosely.

'You must still be very upset by Maggie's death,' said Alison, seizing on what she hoped was the one subject that would divert his mind from money.

'I was shocked, but not particularly upset,' he said. 'She'd changed. Used to be all fun and games. God! The amount of money that harpy took from me, now I think of it. At least you could say she did something for it. It's just fallen into your lap and all you do is screw around with Jenkins.'

'That's not true,' said Alison, her face flaming.

'Aw come *on*, you could hear the pair of you all over the house.'

Alison rounded on him. 'You can't have any money, not ever,' she shouted.

As she ran down the hill, his jeering voice followed her, 'Just mind how you go, sweetie. With you out of the way, there wouldn't be any trouble in us getting our hands on it.'

Alison walked into the house. Donati was in the kitchen, telling off PC Graham. He had just been reminding her it was her duty to keep a watch on Alison and not to sit drinking coffee.

He subjected Alison to another long interview before taking his leave.

Alison went into the sitting room and James Frame rose at her approach. 'Where's Peter?' asked Alison.

'Gone down to the village for cigarettes, I think,' said James. 'I've been wanting to have a talk with you.'

'What about?' asked Alison, although she was sure she knew what was coming.

'Fact is, I need a bit of financial help and wondered if you could let me have a few thou'.'

'No,' said Alison. 'Why should I?'

'Because I think you should pay me back some of the money Maggie got out of me in the past. She was insatiable. The things I had to do to find money to keep her.' His voice took on a faintly cockney whine. 'Come on, darling, you wouldn't miss it.'

'I don't know,' said Alison desperately. 'Leave me alone for just now. In fact, now I think of it, I think you should all leave after the funeral. It's *my* house and I can turn you all out when I want to.'

'Well, that's downright inconsiderate. I took leave and I need a holiday.'

'I shouldn't think you would want to stay under the circumstances.'

'I've got a strong stomach.'

'I'm telling you now,' said Alison as Crispin Witherington walked in. 'You've all got to leave right after the funeral and that's that.'

She walked back to the dining room and stood there, feeling strangely exhilarated. She couldn't remember standing up for herself before.

Then she sensed someone standing behind her and swung round. Crispin Witherington was there, a little smile curving his mouth though his eyes were hard.

'So the chips are down, are they?' he said. 'No money for any of us, except perhaps what Jenkins gets for laying you. Do you know why we all rushed up here? Money. Maggie's money. Do you really think one of us gave a damn for that tart after all those years? She cheated us and conned us rotten and we all wanted some of our money back. It makes me sick to think of a wimp like you with your prissy ways walking off with that old tart's fortune. If I were you, I wouldn't walk along any dark roads for some time to come.'

'Mrs Todd!' screamed Alison.

Both Mrs Todd and Mary Graham erupted into the room as if they had been listening outside the door.

'He threatened me,' said Alison shakily. 'Oh, Mrs Todd, you've got to tell them all to go home after the funeral.' And with that, Alison burst into tears, while PC Graham took out her notebook to question Crispin, and Mrs Todd moved quickly forward, saying, 'Come along, now. You'd best go up to your room and leave us to sort matters out here.'

Alison stumbled out.

But she did not go to her room. She went out to the garage and wrenched open the doors. Driving, that was it, her only solace, her only comfort.

She roared off down the precipitous cliff road, her eyes blurred with tears. The road ran along the edge of the cliff and as Alison raced along, she realized dimly that she was going too fast to take the hairpin bends and pressed on the footbrake. Nothing happened. A corner hurtled towards her and she screeched round it and down the next stretch, her hands sweating on the wheel. Another corner was looming up. She screamed, wrenched into a low gear, and seized the handbrake and pulled with all her might. The car skidded off the road and slithered to a stop, the little front wheels of the mini hanging over the cliff edge.

Alison sat there, numb with shock. Below her the sea heaved and sucked at the base of the cliffs. She gave a whimpering sound and released her seat belt. Although she moved only slightly, the car gave a creak and seemed to dip. She twisted her neck. It was a two-door car and so she could not climb into the back seat and escape that way. It was out of the question to try to struggle through one of the back windows for they were too small and any effort to escape that way might overset the car.

She sat there for what seemed like ages while the screaming seagulls wheeled overhead. The wind was rising, she realized numbly. If she sat there much longer, one good gust would tip the little car into the sea.

Praying loudly, she grasped the door handle and pressed it down. The door swung open. Immediately below her was the sea and just behind, springy turf.

With a yell, she flung herself out of the car, twisting sideways, her fingers scrabbling at the springy turf. She lay face down, her legs dangling over the edge of the cliff. Beside her, with a sad little creak, the mini slowly slid over the edge of the cliff and plunged down into the sea.

Sobbing and grasping grass roots, Alison pulled herself forward on her belly. She heard a car drive up and a car door slam, but still she continued to ease forward until she was well clear of the cliff edge. Then she looked up.

Peter Jenkins was standing there, his hands on his hips, looking down at her.

'Whatever are you doing?' he asked. 'Playing games?'

Hamish Macbeth could never understand why mews cottages, those old converted carriage houses, should be considered chic. They had been built for carriages and coachmen out of the poorest of brick and usually faced north. The cobbled way outside mews cottages always seemed to be a magnet for dog owners who allowed their pets to use it as a lavatory.

The cottage owned by Glenys Evans was painted white and bedecked on the outside with honeysuckle and roses in tubs. Inside it was decorated in neo-Georgian with hunting prints on the walls, fake Chippendale furniture, and a 'Persian' rug made in Belgium on the floor.

Hamish Macbeth was not a sentimental man and did not believe in the fiction of the tart with a heart and Glenys was not of the breed to prove him wrong. She was a thin, stringy woman dressed in tweed skirt, twinset, and pearls. The tarts who squandered their money went down to the gutter and the ones who invested became middle class, thought Hamish, if Glenys and Maggie were anything to go by.

Charm was not going to work with this one and so he did not waste any time in conversation but got down to the interview, asking her respectful questions and calling her ma'am.

Glenys visibly thawed before all this correct courtesy and began to talk about the old days. It was rather like listening to an opera star reminiscing about her heyday, thought Hamish. She talked of the casinos, the private planes, the best hotels, the best restaurants, her eyes filled with happy dreams. Hamish gently steered the conversation round to the four men he was interested in.

'It's all so long ago,' sighed Glenys. 'Let me see, Crispin Witherington.' Her face darkened. 'I remember him. Maggie and I were sharing a flat at the time. He had the nerve to say it was his flat and tried to turn us out. There was ever such a scene. But the deeds to the flat were in Maggie's name whether he paid for it or not. He was only sore because she'd ditched him for that little pipsqueak, James Frame. Now what she ever saw in him, I don't know. Anyway, I remember, she was just getting tired of him when he disappeared from the country. He wrote to say he was bankrupt, I remember. What a laugh we had about that. As Maggie said, it was nothing to do with her. He would have gone bankrupt anyway. Then Steel Ironside. I don't know that much about him. I was living in Cannes with Lord Berringsford at that time, but she was always in the papers. Said they were going to get married. Not her type. But I suppose she enjoyed all the fuss.

Peter Jenkins was soppy about her. Wrote her poetry and turned white when she came into the room. She liked that. We used to have such a giggle. "Here comes love's young dream," I used to say. But this Arab sheik came on the scene and Maggie flipped off with him. She said he was a beast, the sheik, I mean, and she didn't get as much out of him as she had hoped.

'Wait a minute. I might have some photographs.'

Hamish waited patiently while she disappeared upstairs. So much for the fallen woman of Victorian novels, he thought. Glenys showed no signs of being racked with guilt about her past. In fact, she seemed proud of it and obviously thought she had had a successful life which, indeed, in material terms, she had obviously achieved.

She came back downstairs, carrying a box of photographs which she proceeded to rummage through. 'There we both are with Crispin,' she said at last.

Hamish looked at the photograph. Crispin had been a fairly good-looking young man. He was standing with Maggie and Glenys beside a white Rolls Royce. Maggie was slim and blonde and Glenys a sultry brunette. They must have been a formidable pair, thought Hamish. There was a press photograph of Maggie leaving a pop concert with Steel Ironside, a thinner, younger Steel without the beard.

'What happened to her husbands?' asked Hamish suddenly.

'Baird died not long after she married him. He was a stockbroker. Taught her all about the market.'

'What did he die of?'

'Heart attack. He was a lot older than her. The other one, let me see, Balfour, was a bit of a crook. Got done for doing a bank and went inside. Maggie divorced him.'

'What is Balfour's first name and where did he live?'

'His name was Jimmy and he lived in Elvaston Place in Kensington, but I can't remember the number. It wouldn't help you anyway, because he rented the flat and that was years ago.'

'And when did you last see Mrs Baird?'

'The last time I saw her was about a year ago. We didn't part friends. In fact, I gave her a lecture. Letting herself go like that and all over some two-bit waiter. "Get on a diet," I said. "You look a fright, you do."' Glenys patted her bony hips complacently. '"You should be like me,"' I said. '"You've forgotten that men are only good for one thing."'

'Sex?'

Glenys looked amused. 'No, darling, money.'

'What about this waiter?' asked Hamish.

Glenys sighed impatiently and told Hamish as much as she knew about the waiter but said she could not remember either his name or where he had worked but that Maggie had allowed herself to be cheated 'just like a beginner!'

Hamish asked more questions and looked at more photographs, and then finally took his leave. He felt he had learned nothing much to help towards solving the case.

He seemed to have spent hours and hours with Glenys, but he found to his surprise that it was only eleven in the morning and that he had only been with her for an hour. He decided to catch the midday train to Inverness.

During the long journey back north, he kept turning the case over and over in his head. If only Priscilla would call on him, he might be able to see things more clearly. He always did after talking to Priscilla.

But there was no one waiting for him at the police station. Only a note from Alison to say she was staying the night at Mrs Todd's cottage in the village and would he call on her, no matter how late.

Hamish sighed. He hoped it wouldn't turn out to be a waste of time.

There was a constable on duty outside Mrs Todd's cottage, relieving PC Graham. He told Hamish that Alison claimed the brakes of her car had been tampered with and that the mini had ended up in the sea after she had managed to get clear, but that a storm was blowing hard and there was no way they could get the car up until the wind died down.

Hamish knocked on the cottage door and Mrs Todd let him in. 'I told her she was safer here with me rather than staying up there with a houseful of murderers,' she said, 'although I don't know why she wants to see you. She's told that Italian all she knows.'

Mrs Todd led the way into her parlour. It was scrubbed and clean with comfortable old-fashioned furniture. There were several photographs of Mrs Todd in army uniform. She must have been a holy terror, thought Hamish. Alison came down in dressing gown and slippers and Mrs Todd went off into the kitchen to make tea.

Alison looked crushed and subdued. In a little girl voice, she told Hamish about her escape from death, and how Steel, Crispin, and James had all tried to get money out of her. All the while, Hamish was remembering what Glenys had said. He was sure all four men had been genuinely infatuated with Maggie at one time but equally sure that they had never forgiven her for getting their money and then ditching them.

'It couldn't have been Peter, could it?' asked Alison tremulously. 'I mean, he was down in the village getting cigarettes.'

'It's my belief the car's brakes could have been tampered with any time. When did you last use it – I mean before you drove along the cliff?'

'The day before.'

'And it was therefore just lying in the garage where anyone could get to it.'

'I wish Peter were here with me,' said Alison miserably.

'There's nothing to stop you from going back to your own house.'

'It's not that,' said Alison. 'You see, I slept with him.'

'So?'

Alison hung her head. 'A man doesn't respect a girl for just jumping into bed with him when she hardly knows him.'

'That's a pretty old-fashioned way of thinking. Last time I saw you, you looked tae me as if you'd had the experience and enjoyed every minute o' it.'

'Don't!' Alison put up a hand as if to ward him off. 'You men just don't understand.'

Hamish sat up late that night, typing out his report for Donati. He really shouldn't be worrying so much about this case, he chided himself. Donati was highly competent. He would get Scotland Yard to ferret into all the background.

He decided to give his report to Donati first thing in the morning and then go about his village duties and only work on the case when asked to do so, and having come to that decision, he felt much better. Blair's bullying and stupidity in the past was what had spurred him on to all the effort.

He stacked the notes in a neat pile on the

desk and reached over to switch off the lamp when there came a hammering at the door.

Hamish opened it. Detective Jimmy Anderson stood there, his fair hair plastered down by the rain, his face grim.

'Come along, Hamish,' he said. 'There's been another murder.'

'Alison?'

'Naw. That pop singer, Steel Ironside.'

Chapter Eight

Assassination is the extreme form of censorship.
— George Bernard Shaw

Steel Ironside lay across the bed. There was blood everywhere. The meat cleaver which had struck a deep gash right across his neck lay discarded on the floor.

Forensic men were dusting every inch of the room for fingerprints and combing the carpet for signs of clues.

Donati turned and left the room, signalling to Hamish and to the two detectives, MacNab and Anderson, to follow.

'Where are the remaining three guests?' asked Hamish. Donati paused on the stairs. 'They're in the sitting room, waiting to be questioned. Mrs Todd is on her way here with Miss Kerr.'

'A meat cleaver,' said MacNab. 'It must hae been the Todd woman.'

'As far as we know, she didn't leave Lochdubh,' said Donati. 'Her car engine's cold.

Jenkins discovered the body. He said he was uneasy. He said he heard thumping noises coming from Ironside's room and went to investigate. He must have discovered the body minutes after the murder. The body was still warm when we got here.'

He went on down the stairs and the others followed him.

The three men were grouped together in the sitting room. All looked white and strained. Crispin Witherington's eyes were blank with shock, James Frame was hugging himself and shivering, and Peter Jenkins was drinking steadily.

Donati started with Peter. 'If you will just go over it again. You say you heard thumping noises. When was that?'

'I looked at my alarm clock,' said Peter, 'and it was just after one in the morning. I'm upstairs and Steel is ... was ... on the ground floor. Then I thought I heard a door slam. I decided to go down and have a look. I looked in Crispin's bedroom first. I didn't put on the light but I could make out his shape under the bed-clothes in the light from the passage. Then I opened Steel's door.' He gulped. 'I could just make out his figure on the bed but I felt there was something wrong. I don't know why. I switched on the light and saw ... and saw ...'

'All right,' said Donati. 'Take it easy. Now what made you go looking after you heard ... bumps, was it? I mean, what made you think there was something up?'

'I can answer that one,' said Crispin waspishly. 'He thought Alison had returned and gone to bed with one of us and bang goes his millionairess.'

'Is this true?' asked Donati.

'Of course it's not true,' said Peter in a shrill voice. 'I tell you, I can't quite explain it but there was something odd about the sounds. Then I'm sure I heard a door slam, and I wondered if Alison had changed her mind and come home.'

Donati sighed. 'It's a good thing the victim wasn't Miss Kerr or you all might be under suspicion. I gather from PC Graham that both of you, Mr Frame and Mr Witherington, had tried to get money out of her. If she dies, you inherit, and when we get that car of hers up, I'm sure we'll find the brakes were tampered with, that is, if this storm ever dies down.'

There was a silence and all listened as the wind shrieked around the house.

The door opened and Alison came in escorted by Mrs Todd. Alison moved like a sleepwalker. Peter rose to meet her and held out his arms but she shrank away from him.

'Now,' said Mrs Todd, folding her arms, 'which one o' ye has been using my good meat cleaver?'

Hamish had a mad desire to laugh.

'So it was your meat cleaver,' said Donati. 'Sit down, Mrs Todd, and I'll get to you soon. I am going into the study and I'll interview you one by one. MacNab, you stay on duty here. Anderson, come with me and bring your notebook.' He turned to Hamish and said mildly, 'No need for you to stay, Macbeth. The press will be back here in droves tomorrow and they'll be at Mrs Baird's funeral. I'll need you then.'

Hamish walked out of the bungalow. Well, it was what he'd decided, wasn't it? Donati was highly competent and it was a messy murder. But as he drove back to Lochdubh, he could feel anger boiling up in him. Lochdubh was his patch. It was his responsibility to find out the murderer. He was being blinded by Donati's efficiency. Also, it was almost as if Donati had assumed the mantle of Blair and had decided he didn't want Hamish Macbeth on the case. So forget Donati and imagine the man in charge of the case to be Blair. If Blair were on the case, what then would he, Hamish, do?

Keep it very simple, he thought.

He went into the police station and made himself a cup of tea and sat down at the kitchen table. He longed for a cigarette and wondered if the longing would ever go away or whether he would be stuck with it for life.

He went through to the office and got pen and paper and then sat down at the kitchen table again and began to make notes.

He went back to the start of the case. Someone had rigged that Renault to make it burst into flames. Someone had bought a felt mat and spark plugs. The efficient Donati had covered every garage in Sutherland. It was odd that Strathbane should have two detective chief inspectors. It meant that Donati had been recently promoted and Blair should be a very worried man for surely he was due to be demoted so that the police headquarters should have just one of them in charge. Forget Donati. Garages. There might be one somewhere else. There was a shop in Dingwall in the county of Ross and Cromarty which sold motoring accessories. Forget it. Garages and shops in the counties adjoining Sutherland had probably been covered as well. Where else?

Scrap yards. He threw down his pen. There was a sort of graveyard of old cars over at Brora. Anyone wanting cheap spare parts went there. But would four men from London know that?

He picked up the pen again and went on making notes. Gradually his head sank lower. He put his head down on the kitchen table. Just five minutes sleep, that was all . . .

He awoke with a start. Daylight was streaming in the kitchen window. He felt stiff and grimy. He bathed and changed and shaved and went out to feed the hens. Then he got into the Land Rover and drove towards Brora. The funeral was at ten that morning. He must make sure he was back in time for it.

But when he got to the yard it was to find only a mechanic on duty who had recently started work there. The boss, he said, had taken the day off to see friends in Golspie. He'd be back that evening. Hamish stopped off at a phone box in Brora and called Priscilla.

'Look,' he said urgently, 'I wonder if you could do something for me. Will you be at the funeral?'

'Yes,' said Priscilla. 'Daddy's not going. He's getting worse. We still can't find out what's worrying him. What do you want me to do?'

'Do you still have your Polaroid?'

'Yes, it's around here somewhere.'

'I want you to get photographs at the funeral of the four guests and Alison and Mrs Todd.'

'Don't be ridiculous, Hamish!' Priscilla sounded shocked. 'The press will be there in droves and if I start taking pictures as well, they'll think I'm some sort of ghoul.'

'It's awfy important,' pleaded Hamish. 'Tell Alison and anyone else that you are taking the pictures as a memento. Tell them it's an old Highland custom. Tell them anything. Please, Priscilla.'

'Oh, all right,' said Priscilla crossly. 'But if I get into any trouble, I'll blame you.'

The wind had died down and a warm drizzle was falling as Maggie Baird's coffin was lowered into the grave. All the villagers were there as they were at any funeral in Lochdubh. It seemed to Hamish that they were nearly out-numbered by the press. Television vans stood outside the graveyard, photographers perched on the top of tombstones, and reporters in black ties stood respectfully around, although questioning everyone they could get hold of in hushed whispers.

The funeral reception was to be held in the village hall, Mrs Todd and the minister's wife, Mrs Wellington, having decided Alison would not be able to manage the funeral baked meats on her own. Hamish reflected that it might have been better if the organisation of the reception *had* been left to Alison. She looked very frail and she had nothing to take her mind off her fears.

Priscilla was discreetly taking photographs but there were so many press photographers around that no one seemed to notice.

At the funeral reception, she handed Hamish the photographs. 'When this is all over,' said Hamish, 'let's you and me go off somewhere and talk. You're not looking your usual bonny self these days.'

'I'm worried about Daddy,' said Priscilla. 'Yes, I'd like that. The atmosphere at home is all gloom and doom. Did you see Daddy at the funeral? Why on earth did he decide to come along? Thank goodness he didn't stay for the reception. There is so much whisky on offer here and Daddy's been sinking quite a lot of it recently. Look at this photograph. He's standing with Mrs Todd and Alison. See how swollen his face is? He's all bloated up. He won't go to Dr Brodie anymore either.'

Hamish wondered whether to tell Donati

where he was going. But Donati would simply phone the police at Brora and tell Hamish sharply to leave the case alone. Something made Hamish approach Donati and say earnestly, 'I've got some ideas about the case I would like to put to you, sir.'

Donati frowned. 'I haven't time to listen to you at the moment,' he said. 'The press are all over the place. The wind has died down so we've got a chance of getting that car up out of the sea. Just stand by for the moment until I give you your orders.'

Hamish humbly touched his cap and strolled away. He obeyed orders for the rest of the day and even the news that he was to guard the bungalow from the press in the company of PC Graham didn't seem to ruffle him. He stood by one gatepost and PC Graham stood at the other, flashing him an occasional venomous glance. At six o'clock, Hamish looked at his watch and then began to walk off down the drive.

'Hey, you!' yelled Mary Graham. 'Where dae ye think you're going?'

But Hamish did not even turn around.

As he was driving along the waterfront, he saw the gnarled figure of the gardener, Angus Burnside, leaning over the sea wall and drew up.

Angus turned round. 'Ach, what is it noo, Hamish?' he asked crossly. 'I've been answering the polis's questions fur days.'

'Well, humour me, Angus,' said Hamish.

'When you were working around that bungalow, did you see anyone go into that garage
apart from Miss Kerr and Mrs Baird?'

'That wee greaser wi' the uppity manner.'

'Which could apply to all of them,' said
Hamish patiently. 'Which one was it?'

'The smarmy one, him called Witherington.
It wass about twa days afore the death o' Mrs
Baird. "Whit d'ye want?" I went and asked
him, and he got very hoity-toity. "Go back to
your gardening, my good fellow," he says.
Damp English. They should all stay on the
other side o' the border.'

'Anyone else apart from him?'

'Naw, no one but that daftie, Miss Kerr. D'ye
ken, she used tae go and *talk* tae that car!'

Hamish thanked him and drove off on the
long road to Brora again. It was still high summer and in the north of Scotland it hardly ever
gets dark. There was a blazing sunset as he
arrived at the scrap yard. The derelict cars lay
about in various stages of rust and decay. The
purple flowers of the willow herb bloomed
amongst the heaps of twentieth-century junk
and long sour grass sprouted through shattered doors and windows of the less popular
models – less popular for their spare parts. The
whole thing was like a graveyard, a monu-
ment, a tombstone to death on the roads. That
Ford over there, thought Hamish, had anyone
survived that crash? The whole front was
smashed and buckled.

Somewhere a dog howled dismally and the

wind whistled through the rusty cars and swaying grass. At least the rain has stopped, thought Hamish, picking his way round the muddy puddles to a hut in the middle of the yard.

Cars, he thought. This case is all about cars. Forget the meat cleaver for the moment. Cars. Crispin knew about cars. James Frame once worked for him. The others probably knew a bit about car engines. Alison's obsession with driving. What an odd girl she was. Pity she seemed to have taken an aversion to Jenkins. A weak man to look after was just what she needed to stiffen her spine.

There was no one in the hut. Hamish sighed impatiently and sat down in a battered armchair beside the hut door to wait. He was very tired. Poor Priscilla. What on earth could be bothering that father of hers? He couldn't help there. The colonel loathed him. His eyes began to close. Then he heard the sound of a car approaching and straightened up.

The owner of the scrap yard, a small greying man in blue overalls, drove up.

'What do ye want?' he demanded as he approached Hamish. 'There's not one stolen car here.'

Hamish got to his feet. 'I'm not here about stolen cars,' he said. 'I want to show you some photos and I want you to look at the folk in the photos and tell me if one of them called at your yard and asked for an old felt mat, like the kind you see under the bonnets of some engines, and two spark plugs.'

He looked at the man without hope. It was too long a shot. 'Funny that,' said the owner slowly. 'I call to mind someone asking me for thae things.'

Hamish held out the photographs.

The man took them and led the way into the hut. He switched on the light and then with maddening slowness took a pair of glasses from his overall pocket and put them on his nose. He peered at the photographs.

'Aye,' he said. 'That's who ye want.'

Hamish looked down. His finger was almost covering one face.

'My God!' said Hamish. 'Are ye sure? Ye have to be awfy sure. If it's that one, man, I couldnae for the life o' me think why.'

'Of course I'm sure,' he said testily. 'I can call tae mind every sod that comes in here. Came and asked fur spark plugs and then fur the felt tae line the bonnet o' a car. A Renault it was.'

Hamish took out a form he had brought with him and took down a statement and got the scrap yard owner to sign it. As he drove off, the sun was slipping below the horizon and the perpetual twilight of a northern summer lay across the countryside.

He drove a little way and pulled off the road and sat, thinking hard. Why?

And then, after an hour, all the little bits and pieces fell into place and he was looking at an almost complete picture. There was only one large piece missing and that was the reason for the death of Steel Ironside.

He called first at Dr Brodie's, then at the minister's, back to the police station to make a few phone calls, and then made his way to the bungalow. PC Graham was still on duty. 'You're going to cop it frae Donati,' she jeered, 'and I'm coming in tae watch.'

Hamish ignored her and went on into the house. Mrs Todd was busy at the kitchen sink. 'They're all in the sitting room,' she said.

Hamish walked into the sitting room. Crispin, Peter, and James were sitting together on the sofa. Alison was curled up in an armchair. Donati was sitting on a hard chair in the middle. MacNab and Anderson were over by the window.

Donati looked up briefly and his face hardened. 'I'll deal with you later, Macbeth,' he said. 'Get outside and make sure no press get as far as the house.'

'But –' began Hamish.

'I said, get outside!'

PC Graham sniggered and took up a position against the wall, anxious to stay and watch the interrogation. Hamish could stand guard on his own.

Hamish did not go outside. He went into the kitchen and pulled out a kitchen chair and sat down.

In his usual lazy, companionable way, he said, 'Aye, it was a grand funeral. A fitting funeral for a lady like Mrs Baird.'

Mrs Todd said nothing but continued to scrub pots with ferocious energy.

'She was a verra good woman as well,' Hamish went on.

Mrs Todd swung round. 'Maggie Baird was a whore,' she said viciously.

Hamish gave a little sigh and said quietly, 'And you are the instrument of God.'

She wiped her hands on her apron and slowly came and sat down opposite him. Hamish clasped his hands behind his head and looked dreamily at the ceiling. 'It was those photographs of you in the army. You were in the army during the war and would know a lot about car engines. You were a chauffeur to a Colonel Wilson in the Royal Artillery, or so the village gossip goes. You burned that book of Maggie's. You read it and you burned it. I gather from Alison it was pretty hot stuff. Enough to turn that daft mind o' yours.

'Your husband took to the drink and you joined the Temperance Society and you neffer gave the man a day's peace till he drank himself to death. You asked Brodie to put "heart attack" on the death certificate because you thought alcohol poisoning was a disgrace. He refused, but it was what else Brodie told you that shocked you. He told you your husband had venereal disease. Brodie told me that Mr Todd had confessed to going with prostitutes from time to time in Aberdeen because he had had nothing in that line from you since your wedding night. Then I remembered the case of Mary MacTavish. She had an illegitimate child and Mr Wellington said you made that lassie's life such hell she had to leave the village. When the minister reproached you for your lack of charity, you said you were doing God's work.

'Now, we come to Alison Kerr.

'She was a girl after your own heart, quiet and shy. But I gather you can hear everything in this house and so you listened at her bedroom door and that way you found out she was in bed with Peter Jenkins. You had committed murder once. And to my mind it was murder. You knew Maggie Baird had a weak heart. So you tampered with the brakes of Alison's car. She had become unclean and had to go. But when you managed to poison her mind against Peter Jenkins . . . oh, I'm sure that rubbish Alison was talking about that a man would never respect you after you had slept with him came from you . . . I think you decided to give her a reprieve. Then the pop singer. You didn't use the car but you could easily have cycled out or walked.'

'You can't prove a thing,' said Mrs Todd.

'Oh, but I can,' said Hamish, straightening up, his eyes hard and implacable and cold. 'You went to the scrap yard at Brora and got the spark plugs and the bit o' felt and the man there identified you from your photograph.'

Mrs Todd rose and went back to the sink and started scrubbing pots again.

'I'll tell you something else,' said Hamish. 'You're like Maggie Baird.'

Mrs Todd stopped scrubbing. 'Never!' she said passionately.

'Yes, in a way. You see, when Maggie was all fat and tweedy and playing the county lady, I had an odd feeling that there was a pretty, flirtatious woman locked up inside all that fat, ready to come out like a butterfly coming out of a chrysalis. Inside that motherly outside of yours, Mrs Todd, I see another woman: a thin, sharp, bitter, murderous woman.'

'Havers,' said Mrs Todd calmly and opened a kitchen drawer.

Detective Jimmy Anderson was to say long afterwards that the biggest shock he ever had in his career was when Hamish Macbeth erupted from that kitchen and dived over the sofa and the three men sitting on it, pursued by Mrs Todd who was waving a glittering bread knife. Galvanized into action, MacNab and Anderson and Donati grabbed hold of her while PC Graham twisted the bread knife out of her hand. She struggled and cursed, trying to escape, her eyes bulging with hate as she surveyed the lanky length of Hamish Macbeth rising from behind the sofa.

As they put the handcuffs on her, Hamish charged her with the attempted murder of Mrs Margaret Baird. Then he said, 'Why Steel Ironside? Why the pop singer?'

'Dirty man!' Mrs Todd spat out the words. 'He wore his shirts open the whole time show-ing all that nasty, nasty hair. Yes, I burned that book of hers. I knew men were filth but I never realized how filthy till I read it. Wallowing in filth. Filth!' she screamed, and she was still screaming while they led her outside.

'She's mad,' whispered Alison.

'Yes,' said Hamish wearily. 'Barking mad and I never even noticed.'

'Yaas,' said James in his fake upper-class voice. 'Of course, one never really looks at servants. I say, Alison, what about drinks all round? Thank God it's all over.'

'Yes,' said Alison, a little colour beginning to come into her pale face. 'Yes, it's over and I'm safe.' She flung her arms around Hamish. 'Oh, thank you!'

Hamish looked across her head to Peter Jenkins and signalled with his eyes and Peter came up. Hamish pushed Alison gently into Peter's arms. 'I'd best be off,' he said.

He had parked his Land Rover on the road outside. The press had disappeared for the moment but he knew they would soon be back. PC Graham was standing morosely on duty.

'I suppose you think you're damned clever,' she sneered.

Hamish looked at her, at the thin mouth and at the dislike in her eyes.

'You look beautiful when you're angry,' he said. He jerked her into his arms and kissed her on the mouth. Then he walked off whistling.

Her voice followed him. 'Why, Hamish! I never knew ... I never guessed. Hamish, darling ...'

Hamish threw one horrified look behind him and then ran to his Land Rover and drove off, breaking the speed limit all the way to Lochdubh.

At the police station, he fed Towser, locked up the hens for what was left of the night, and started to make himself some supper. And then the bell at the police station door sounded.

He walked up to it and shouted, 'No comment' through the letter box.

'It's me, Donati,' said a voice.

Hamish opened the door.

Donati walked past him and into the police office. 'I'll need your notes, Macbeth. Was it a lucky guess?'

'No, I hae proof.' Hamish fished in his pocket and brought out the statement by the owner of the scrap yard along with the photographs. Then he outlined what he had found out about Mrs Todd's background.

'I should say "good work",' said Donati crisply, 'but we could have found all this out much sooner if you had confided in me.'

'But I only got the proof this evening,' said Hamish.

'So you say. Well, type up your notes and let me have them along with this statement and the photographs. I shall be at the hotel until lunchtime tomorrow.'

'Very well,' said Hamish.

'Very well, what?'

'Very well, *sir*,' said Hamish, resisting a longing to tell Donati exactly what he thought of him. But Donati might make things hot for him at headquarters in Strathbane and they might close down the police station again.

After Donati had left, he typed up his notes and put everything in an envelope.

The next morning, Donati simply took the envelope without a word of thanks. 'We are now leaving for Strathbane,' said Donati. 'They will be raising that mini today. The divers will be along, but Anderson here will be in charge of that so there is nothing to take you away from your village duties.'

Jimmy Anderson gave Hamish a sympathetic wink.

Hamish left the hotel and walked along the waterfront. The day was sunny and mild. Terror and murder had left the village. Mrs Todd had been among them all for so long and yet none of them had realized she was unbalanced. But there were so many oddities in any village and no one ever stopped to wonder overmuch about them. There were at least four religious maniacs in Lochdubh apart from Mrs Todd, and that was a small number for the Highlands where old-fashioned Calvinists still abounded and nothing moved on a Sunday for fear of incurring the wrath of God.

He took a deck chair out into the garden, stretched out in the sun, and fell asleep.

PC Macbeth had returned to his normal village duties.

Chapter Nine

Poverty is an anomaly to rich people. It is very difficult to make out why people who want dinner do not ring the bell.
— Walter Bagehot

As the shadows of violent murder withdrew from the village of Lochdubh, the weather took a turn for the better and long, lazy, hot days sent mist curling up from the sea loch and the mountains stood out stark and awesome against the bluest of skies. Purple heather blazed in all its glory on the hillsides and moorland and children collected wild raspberries from the hedgerows. The whole world seemed to have slowed almost to a halt as the sleepy village sank into a sunlit torpor.

Hamish was happy. Two whole weeks had passed since the murder and already it was fading from his mind. He had heard that Crispin and James had left the bungalow but that Peter Jenkins had stayed on, which explained, thought Hamish, why he had not been pestered by Alison. He had caught a fleeting glimpse of her when Peter had driven her through the village. He would have expected Alison to have bought another car, but perhaps the obsession for motoring had left her.

And then into this idyllic peace and quiet came Detective Chief Inspector Blair. Hamish was weeding the garden when the bulky shadow of Blair fell across him.

He straightened up, waiting for the inevitable remarks about lazy coppers but Blair surprised him by saying mildly, 'Care tae come along tae the hotel for a drink, Hamish?'

'Sure,' said Hamish, surprised. 'I'll be with you in a tick. Just got to wash my hands.'

He went indoors and quickly washed and scrambled into his uniform. Blair must be on a case. He could hardly have come all the way from Strathbane to pass the time of day.

They walked along together to the hotel, but Blair seemed to be reluctant to get to the point of his visit. He asked questions about the fishing and was it any good and then barely seemed to hear Hamish's replies. Once they were seated in a corner of the hotel bar, Hamish said, 'Well, what's the case?'

'What? Oh, ah, I amnae on a case, Hamish. Fine day. Jist popped over to hae a wee chat.'

'About what?' asked Hamish suspiciously.

'That nasty bugger, Donati.'

'Oh, him,' said Hamish. 'What about him?'

'Well, I had it frae Anderson and MacNab that it was you that solved the murder case.'

'You would get that from Donati's report,' said Hamish sharply.

'Not a bit o' it.'

'I saw the newspapers crediting him with solving the murder,' said Hamish, 'but I didn't think a man like Donati would take all the credit back at headquarters.'

Blair gave him a long, bleak look.

Hamish shifted uncomfortably. 'Now I come to think of it, that's what he *would* do.'

'Aye, I got a look at his report. He said he had sent an officer, no name mentioned, to a scrap yard in Brora with photographs o' the suspects and thereby had obtained proof o' the Todd woman's guilt. When Anderson and MacNab finally told me, I felt it my duty to go to the super.'

Hamish grinned. 'It must hae choked ye to give me any praise.'

'I'm a fair man,' said Blair huffily. 'But the super said that Donati's success had given him the transfer to Glasgow C.I.D. that he'd been angling after and it would rock the boat to start accusations flying around at this late date. So that scunner, Donati, went off south yesterday. Made my life a misery while he was in Strathbane. When they made him detective chief inspector, too, I knew it would only be a matter o' time before they demoted me.'

'Then it's all to the good,' said Hamish. 'It's one way of getting rid of him. Thanks for telling me, anyway.'

'I put the super's back up, ye see, because o' that Graham woman. The bitch. I really thought you'd gone off your trolley, Hamish, and assaulted her.'

His voice was wheedling and conciliatory. Hamish looked at him sharply. Blair had been plotting his downfall for years. What was behind it all?

'So I hae been thinking ... another drink, Hamish?'

'Yes, thank you. Whisky again, please.'

Blair came back, carrying two doubles. Hamish blinked at this unusual generosity.

'So you didn't come all this way to tell me what you could hae told me on the phone,' said Hamish. 'What do you want?'

'It's like this.' Blair hitched his chair closer to Hamish. 'Ye seem tae attract murder. Now, say you get another big crime up here, I would be obliged if you could ask Strathbane for me.'

'Oh.' Hamish leaned back and studied Blair thoughtfully. 'Why should I do that? At least Donati let me in on most of the case. You always send me off wi' a flea in my ear.'

'Stands tae reason,' blustered Blair. 'You're only the village copper. Look! I promise to let ye in on the ground floor next time. Hae another drink.'

'I haven't started this one yet. So what's behind it all?' Hamish looked at the big detective thoughtfully. Then he gave a slow smile. 'Donati's gone. But there's another bright spark climbing up the ranks. Who is it?'

196

'This wee bastard, Finnock. Slimy wee bug-ger wi' a face like an arse,' said Blair viciously. 'It's yes, Mr Daviot, and certainly, sir, and here are some flowers frae my garden fur your wife, sir, and lick your bum, sir. Yuch!'

'And I thought you were the best crawler in the business,' said Hamish. Blair looked about to explode so he said placatingly, 'Okay. I'll ask for you next time. But believe me, there cannae be a next time or we'll be changing the name o' the place from Lochdubh to Murder Village!'

After Blair had finally driven off, Hamish returned to the police station. He was not used to drinking so much whisky in the middle of the day and he felt quite lightheaded.

He saw Alison and Peter Jenkins waiting outside the police station and turned to flee but it was too late. Alison had seen him.

As he approached the couple, he found he was staring at Alison in surprise. Her hair was shining and groomed in a new feathery cut. Gone were the thick glasses. She was expertly made up and she was wearing a blue cotton blouse and a pair of hot pants which revealed that she had very good legs indeed.

'Hey, Hamish!' said Alison cheerfully. 'We've come to say goodbye.'

'Come inside and I'll make some tea,' said Hamish. 'Where are you going?'

'I'm putting that bungalow up for sale. Peter and I are getting married.' She held out a slim hand to show a diamond engagement ring.

'Congratulations!' said Hamish. Peter smiled modestly as if he had done something very clever.

'Where are you going to live?' asked Hamish, putting on the kettle.

'In London,' said Alison. 'Maggie owned a flat in Mayfair, in Charles Street. We're moving there. Peter wants to build up his advertising agency but I said to him, why bother? I mean, I've enough for both of us.'

'It'll certainly be pleasant to be a gentleman of leisure,' drawled Peter.

As Alison talked, Hamish watched her animated face. She and Peter would travel. There were so many countries she wanted to see.

Another butterfly, thought Hamish. It takes a weak man to make a strong woman. Alison was the one who was making all the decisions. Now that she was no longer interested in him, Hamish found her likeable.

'You haven't said anything about a new car,' he said. 'There certainly wasn't much of your mini left by the time they got it out to find the brakes had been tampered with.'

'I don't want to drive anymore,' said Alison with a shudder. 'Peter can do all the driving from now on.'

When they left, Hamish hoped Alison would manage to keep her fortune. A million pounds was no longer what it used to be and could be dissipated in an amazingly short space of time.

He was just settling down to enjoy some peace and quiet when he sensed an unease outside. He couldn't quite place it, but it was as if something bad had happened to alarm the village. He went round to his front garden and leaned on the fence.

Agnes, one of the maids from Tommel Castle, was coming along the main street. She stopped to talk to the Currie sisters and Hamish heard the sisters' sharp exclamations of surprise and dismay.

Not another murder, he thought.

Agnes came nearer and he went to meet her. 'What's happened?' he asked.

'It's himself. The colonel,' gasped Agnes. 'Called us all together last night and said he'd have to fire us all. He's lost all his money! What do you think happened?'

But Hamish was off and running for the Land Rover.

The castle door was open and Hamish walked in. Priscilla was crossing the hall. She stopped short at the sight of him and then she began to cry in a helpless way.

He put his arms around her and held her close, stroking her hair. When she had calmed down, he led her into the drawing room and sat down on the sofa with her, a comforting arm around her shoulders.

'What exactly happened?' he asked. 'Agnes says he fired all the staff last night.'

'Yes. He . . . he . . . called Mummy and me into the study and told us what was worrying him. As he talked, he got into one of his rages and I was afraid he might have a stroke. I feel so guilty.' She dried her eyes firmly and gave a pathetic hiccup.

Mrs Halburton-Smythe came into the room and stopped short at the sight of Hamish. Then she came forward and sat down, looking helplessly at him. 'What are we to do, Hamish?' she said. There were two spots of colour on her pale cheeks and, unlike her daughter, she looked angry. 'How could he do this to us?'

'Do what?' asked Hamish sharply.

Priscilla twisted her wet handkerchief in her hands. 'That's why I feel so guilty,' she said. 'If it hadn't been for me this would never have happened. Do you remember John Harrington?'

'Your boyfriend who got done for insider trading? Yes.'

'It turns out he had persuaded Daddy to let him have a vast sum to invest. Well, he didn't invest it. He skipped bail and the country with it.'

'We've got nothing at all,' said Mrs Halburton-Smythe. 'Nothing.'

'Oh, dear.' Hamish looked about him. 'But you have the castle, and the estates alone must be worth a fortune.'

'Yes, but everything costs a fortune to run,' said Priscilla. 'We can sell it. We have to sell it.

But we're letting down the locals. Most of the staff apart from Jenkins, the butler, come in daily from the village but they rely on us for work. Daddy decided to fire the lot of them, not to mention the gamekeepers and gardeners and water bailiffs. We tried to tell him that somehow the place would need to be kept going until we could find a buyer, but he wouldn't listen.'

Hamish thought quickly. 'You might not have to sell it,' he said.

Priscilla's mother looked at him in anguish. 'Don't be stupid,' she wailed. 'Haven't we just told you we can't afford to run it?'

'There's a way you could,' said Hamish, 'and keep the staff. Where is the colonel?'

'In his study,' said Priscilla. 'But don't bother him, Hamish. The last person he will want to see is you.'

'Be back in a minute,' said Hamish with a grin. 'I think he'll listen to me.'

Mrs Halburton-Smythe made a halfhearted attempt to stop him and then sank helplessly back in her chair.

Hamish went across the hall to the study and went in without knocking. Colonel Halburton-Smythe looked up and a purplish colour rose in his cheeks.

'Get out of here!' he roared. 'Can't you see I've got enough to worry me without listening to the ditherings and bletherings of the village idiot?'

For one blissful minute, Hamish imagined how lovely it would be to tell the old horror to go to hell and fry. But then he thought of Priscilla. He pulled out a chair and sat down and smiled amiably at the colonel.:

'I hae thought o' a grand way in which you could keep this house and the estates and the staff.'

The colonel looked at him in silence, his eyes popping. Then he shrugged. 'You're mad,' he said.

'No, just listen. You've got grand fishing and shooting here,' said Hamish. 'Run it as a hotel. Wi' the shooting and the fishing, you could charge top rates. You've got a lot of bedrooms and most of them have their own bathroom.'

The colonel stared at Hamish in silence, his small mouth hanging slightly open.

There was a soft knock at the door which then opened and Priscilla and her mother came into the study, both fearful in case Hamish's visit was driving the colonel into an apoplexy.

'Are you all right, dear?' asked the colonel's wife timidly. The colonel waved a peremptory hand for silence and sat staring off into the distance.

'What did you say?' whispered Priscilla fiercely in Hamish's ear. 'He looks worse. He looks as if he has had a terrible shock.'

The colonel suddenly brought both of his small plump hands down on the desk with a thump that made them all jump.

'I've found a way to save Tommel Castle,' he said.

'How? How can we?' gasped Mrs Halburton-Smythe.

'We'll open it up as a hotel,' said the colonel triumphantly. 'Think of it. With the best shooting and the best fishing here, we'll make a fortune. We can invite our friends –'

'No,' said Hamish quickly. 'No friends. Mark my words, they'll look offended when you hand them the bill.'

'Don't interrupt,' snapped the colonel. 'I have to make plans. Priscilla, get that secretary of mine here and get that architect chappie over from Strathbane.'

'Do you think it will work?' asked Priscilla cautiously. 'I mean, have we enough to keep going until we open for business?'

'Of course it will work,' said her father robustly. 'We've just enough to manage on until then. Trust me to come up with something. My chaps in the regiment always relied on me. Always a good man for thinking up ways out of a scrape. That was me.'

Priscilla glanced at Hamish, who gave her a limpid look.

'Well, dear,' said Mrs Halburton-Smythe, 'I am sure we are all grateful to Hamish for –'

'Stop wittering, woman, and tell the staff they can stay. Priscilla, get that architect on the phone. And you, Macbeth, have you nothing better to do?'

'I'm off,' said Hamish cheerfully. 'Grand to see you're your old horrible self.'

Priscilla followed him out. 'Honestly,' she said furiously. 'Daddy is the uttermost limit. That was your idea, Hamish.'

'So long as you're all happy,' said Hamish amiably. 'I chust hope I haff not messed up your own career. I mean, surely they won't expect you to work in the hotel.'

'They won't. But I'm going to,' said Priscilla. 'Can you imagine Daddy as mine host, Hamish? He'll forget they're paying guests and start insulting them!'

'I wass going to point out to him that he could have sold off his estates and kept the castle,' said Hamish.

'It wouldn't have done any good. He wants to keep everything and you've found him a way to do it.'

'Aye, that's what I thought. So long as he remembers that a hotel keeper can't go on like the lord of the manor.'

'I doubt if he'll remember it for a moment,' said Priscilla. 'I'll probably have to run it myself and let him think he's doing it all on his own.'

'You really don't mind?'

'Not really, Hamish. I was getting tired of London anyway.'

'And I hope you don't feel guilty anymore,' said Hamish. 'Anyone daft enough to trust a rat like Harrington would be bound to lose their money to some fool sooner or later . . . or their heart.'

Priscilla's cheeks turned pink. 'That's below the belt, Hamish.'

'Perhaps.'

'Is Alison staying on in Lochdubh?' asked Priscilla, deliberately changing the subject.

'No, she's getting married to Peter and they're going to live in London. Let's hope that's the last of crime in Lochdubh.' He told her about his visit from Blair.

'I don't think you're cut out to be a policeman,' said Priscilla. 'You let these detectives walk all over you. And for what? So that you can stay on as village constable and do as little as possible.'

'That's right,' said Hamish amiably.

'You are infuriating. Why don't you come in on this hotel lark?' She walked out of the hall with him and across the drive to the police Land Rover.

Hamish raised his hands in mock horror. 'Tae my mind, working for your dad would be worse than working for Blair any day. What's the matter, Priscilla? Don't you like me the way I am?'

She looked down thoughtfully at her sandalled feet and did not reply

'Well, cheerio,' said Hamish. 'See you around.'

'Hamish, I . . .'

'Yes?' He turned around.

'Nothing,' mumbled Priscilla.

As Hamish drove down to the police station, he found he was feeling very happy indeed, almost elated. It could surely not be because a moneyless, hotel-owning, working Priscilla was within his reach.

No, he told himself, that nonsense was over, but happiness bubbled inside him. He felt sure the days of crime were over for Lochdubh, and Priscilla would be just up the road all year round.

In the evening, he realized he had forgotten to buy anything for his dinner. He had sent, as usual, a good part of his monthly wage back to his mother and father and brothers and sisters over in Cromarty and so he could not afford to dine at the hotel. He ransacked his cupboards and came up with a solitary tin of baked beans.

'Beans it'll have tae be,' he said to Towser. 'And no butcher's meat for you tonight, my boy. Dog food's all we've got.' Towser hung his head and glared at the linoleum.

The phone rang. Hamish put down the cans and went to answer it. The caller was Priscilla.

'Hamish,' she said. 'There are a few points about this hotel business we would like to discuss with you. Could you possibly come to dinner this evening? Just the family and don't dress. You can even bring Towser.'

Hamish accepted the invitation. He put down the phone and grinned at the receiver. 'The auld man must hae been at the whisky,' he said to Towser who had followed him. 'Dinner at the castle for us. Come along.'

He put on a clean shirt and tie and a pair of new trousers. He gave Towser a quick brush and then led the dog out to the police Land Rover.

'Times are changing, Towser,' said Hamish Macbeth as he drove through the heathery twilight.

If you enjoyed *Death of a Hussy,* read on for the first chapter of the next book in the *Hamish Macbeth* series . . .

DEATH
of a SNOB

Chapter One

Heap on more wood! – the wind is chill;
But let it whistle as it will;
We'll keep our Christmas merry still.
                              – Sir Walter Scott

Police Constable Hamish Macbeth was a desperate man – ill, friendless, and, at the approach to Christmas, near to death.

Or so he told himself.

The start of the misery had been the beginning of a Scottish winter which seemed hell-bent on proving any scientist believing in the greenhouse effect a fool. Like many others in the village of Lochdubh on the west coast of Sutherland, Hamish had contracted a severe cold with all its attendant miseries of boiling head, running nose, aching joints and monumental self-pity. Although he had not phoned anyone to tell of his misery, nevertheless, like all people in the grip of self-pity, he expected his friends to have telepathic powers.

The only bright spark in all the gloom was that he was going home for Christmas. His parents had moved to a croft house and land near Rogart. He would soon be there, with his mother to fuss over him.

He was hunched up in his bed. He was hungry and thirsty but could not be bothered getting up to get himself anything. His dog Towser, a yellowish mongrel, lay stretched out at the end of his bed, snoring happily and apparently as indifferent as the rest of Lochdubh to the long lank bundle of misery that was PC Macbeth.

The wind of Sutherland, always savage, had taken on a new dark intensity and boomed down the sea loch outside, bearing long snaking writhing arms of fine snow, tearing at the fabric of the house, yelling and shouting in triumph.

And then suddenly, the phone in the police station office began to ring, sharp and insistent. He hoped no one had committed a crime. He felt too ill to cope, but if he did not attend to the matter himself, Sergeant MacGregor would have to travel all the way from Cnothan, and the peeved sergeant would then set about making trouble for him at police headquarters in Strathbane. He shoved his feet into a battered pair of carpet slippers and, snivelling dismally, he went through to the cold office and picked up the phone.

'Hamish,' came his mother's voice, 'I've got bad news.'

His heart gave a lurch. 'Are you all right?' he asked. 'Nothing up with Faither?'

'No, no, son. It's about Christmas.'

'What about Christmas?' Hamish had a bleak feeling that whatever his mother had to tell him about Christmas was not going to cheer him one bit.

'Well, Aunt Hannah's coming all the way from America. Sprung it on us at the last minute.'

Hamish gripped the phone and stifled a sneeze. Aunt Hannah was a fat, loud-mouthed harridan who loathed Hamish. But she had been generous to the not-too-comfortably-off Macbeths with presents of money and gifts for Hamish's little brothers and sisters. Never anything for Hamish. She loathed him and never tired of saying so.

His mother's voice grew plaintive, 'So you see, son, after all Hannah's done for us and her coming all this way to see us . . .'

There was another long silence.

At last Hamish said bleakly, 'You don't want me to come.' It was not a question.

'I knew you'd understand,' pleaded his mother. 'I mean, it's only this one Christmas. You could come at the New Year when she's gone.'

'Aye, all right,' muttered Hamish.

'I mean,' coaxed Mrs Macbeth, 'you've got lots o' friends in Lochdubh. Your voice sounds funny.'

'I haff got the influenza,' said Hamish, his Highland accent growing more sibilant, a sure sign he was upset.

'Och,' said Mrs Macbeth with all the heart-lessness of a busy mother with a large family, 'you always did think you were dying when you got a wee bit o' a cold. Take some aspirin and go to bed.'

Another silence. 'Wass there anything else?' Hamish finally asked in accents as chilly as the police office.

'No, no, that was all. Sorry, son, but you know how Hannah is. Ever since you put that mouse down her back when you were eight, she's never been fond o' you. The new house is just fine. Rare and warm. The fires draw just grand.'

'When's Aunt Hannah arriving?' asked Hamish.

'On the twentieth.'

'Provided I am still alive,' said Hamish stiffly, 'I'll run over with your presents before then.'

'Aye, that'll be great. See you then.'

Hamish shuffled back miserably to bed. No one wanted him. He was alone in the world. He was dying and nobody cared.

There came a sharp rap at the back door. He sneezed dismally and stayed where he was. Towser stirred lazily and slowly wagged his tail. The rapping came louder now, more peremptory.

Hamish's conscience gave him a nudge. He was Lochdubh's only policeman, the weather was savage, and someone out there might be in trouble. He groaned as he got up again, slung an old woollen dressing-gown about his shoulders, and made his way to the kitchen door.

He opened it and Priscilla Halburton-Smythe was borne in on a gust of wind and snow.

'Oh, it's yerself, Priscilla,' said Hamish.

Priscilla, once the love of his life, until Hamish had grown heartily sick of the weight of the torch he was carrying for her, slammed the door on the storm and looked at Hamish.

'I know crime's thin on the ground here at the best of times,' she said briskly, 'but it's two in the afternoon and you've obviously just got out of bed.'

'I am a sick man,' said Hamish furiously, 'but a fat lot you care. You never even thought to phone.'

'How on earth was I supposed to know you were sick?' asked Priscilla. She looked slowly around the kitchen, at the cold stove, at the dirty pots and dishes piled up in the sink. 'This place is enough to make anyone ill. For heaven's sake, get back to bed and leave me to clear up this mess.'

'Couldn't you chust make us a cup of tea and come and sit by the bed and talk to me?' moaned Hamish.

'Nonsense. You'll feel miles better when this place is spick and span.' Priscilla radiated nervous energy. She had grown thin and spare and her hair was scraped up in an untidy knot on the top of her head. Hamish thought that since her family home, Tommel Castle, had been turned into an hotel, she had not once relaxed. Although her father, Colonel Halburton-Smythe, owned the hotel, all the work fell on Priscilla. As there was excellent fishing and shooting, it was busy even in winter. It was Priscilla who saw to everything, from ordering the food and drink to soothing down the guests offended by her father's blunt manner. In an amazingly short time, she had made a success of the business, but she had lost her cool good looks and graceful movements; perpetually worried, perpetually strung up, now brittle to snapping point.

Hamish crept back to bed. 'What a pigsty!' exclaimed Priscilla, following him in. 'Have you fed Towser?'

'Just some o' the hard food. He doesnae like it owermuch.'

'He never did like it. He likes people food. You know that, Hamish. Come, Towser.'

Towser slid off the bed and crept servilely after her.

Hamish lay listening to the sound of Priscilla scrubbing floors and cleaning out cupboards and washing dishes. He felt she ought to be at his bedside, stroking his brow, instead of going on like some sort of health visitor.

Two hours later, she crashed into the bedroom, carrying a bucket and mop and dusters. She raked out the fire, which was choked with cold ashes, piled it up with paper and wood, and set a cheerful blaze crackling. 'I've run you a hot bath,' she said over her shoulder. 'Go and take it while I change your bed.'

'I think I'm too ill to take a bath.'

'Take it,' she ordered, 'and stop being so disgustingly sorry for yourself.'

'Haff I complained?' Hamish gave her thin back a wounded look.

'You are exuding such self-pity, it's creeping like smoke through the whole place. *Go on!*'

Injured, Hamish stalked off to the bathroom. With quick nervous movements, Priscilla stripped the sheets off the bed and replaced them with clean ones. She dusted and vacuumed the room and then made up a flask of tea and put it, along with a cup, at Hamish's bedside.

Hamish emerged from his bath to find Priscilla waiting to settle him in bed. She neatly arranged the blankets over him and then tucked them in all round him, so firmly he felt he was in a straitjacket.

'There's tea in that flask,' said Priscilla, 'and a casserole on the stove for your dinner. Towser's been fed.'

Hamish wriggled his toes and eased the tight blankets a bit. The fire was roaring up the chimney and the room looked clean and comfortable and there was a delicious smell coming from the kitchen. He began to feel better.

'I'd better be off,' sighed Priscilla. 'I didn't mean to be here so long.'

'Thank you,' said Hamish awkwardly, and then blurted out before he could stop himself, 'My, lassie, but you're awf'y thin.'

Priscilla sat down on the end of the bed. 'I know,' she said. 'And to think that before Daddy started the hotel, I was considering going on a diet.'

'If he looks after the money this time instead of handing it over to some con man,' – Priscilla winced, said con man having been one of her boyfriends – 'he should be able to take down that hotel sign soon and return to being a private landowner.'

'He enjoys it all,' said Priscilla sadly. 'He's having the time of his life.'

'Yes, I have seen him.' Hamish looked at her sympathetically. 'You run yourself ragged with all the management and bookings and complaints while he puts on a black tie in the evening and lords it over the guests. Then he has a few and forgets they're paying guests and is nasty to them, and you have to soothe them down.'

'I'll manage.'

'You don't need to,' said Hamish. 'Things are going just fine. Why, he could hire an experienced hotel manager and give you a break.'

'But no one else could handle the guests the way I can,' protested Priscilla.

'Once the colonel was paying someone to run things, he might mind his tongue. It's because you're his daughter and a woman that he treats you like a skivvy.'

'It's not as bad as that.' Priscilla rose to go.

'Well, it was nice of you to come and look after me.'

Priscilla turned pink. 'I didn't know you were ill, Hamish. There's another reason.'

'Oh, aye? I should hae known,' he said huffily. 'Out with it.'

'There's this friend of mine staying at the hotel. She's leaving at the end of the week. She's got a bit of a problem and doesn't want to go to the police direct, if you know what I mean. She just wants some advice. Could you see her? I'd rather she told you about it.'

'Oh, all right. Bring her down tomorrow. What's her name?'

'Jane. Jane Wetherby.'

The next day, the snow stopped and a mild gale blew in from the Atlantic, turning the snow to slush. For a brief few hours, a watery sunlight shone on the choppy waters of the loch before night fell, as it does in the far north of Scotland in winter, at two in the afternoon.

Hamish was feeling considerably better. He received a phone call from headquarters at Strathbane reminding him that he was expected to stop motorists at random and breathalyze them as part of a campaign to stop drunk driving over Christmas. Hamish, who knew every drunk in the village and solved the problem by taking their car keys away, had no intention of wasting time breathalyzing the rest of the population.

He ate lunch, fed his hens, gave his sheep their winter feed, and then climbed back into bed with a book. He had completely forgotten about Priscilla's friend. Lulled by a glass of toddy, his eyes were beginning to close when he heard a car driving up.

Then he remembered about Jane Wetherby. It was too late to get dressed. He rose and tied his dressing-gown about him and made for the kitchen door, exuding a strong smell of whisky and winter green.

'Be back for Jane later,' called Priscilla. 'I'll leave you to it.'

Hamish ushered Jane into the kitchen and then looked at her in startled amazement as she removed her coat and threw it on a kitchen chair. She was a tall woman wearing a brief divided skirt in shocking-pink wool, and her long, long legs ended in high-heeled sandals with thin patent-leather straps. Her thin white blouse plunged at the front to a deep V. Hamish cast a wild look through the kitchen window as if to reassure himself that the weather had not turned tropical, and then took in the rest of her. She had cloudy dark hair and very large grey-green eyes, a straight thin nose, and a long thin upper lip over a small pouting lower lip.

'Well, well,' said Jane in a sort of breathy voice, 'so you're the village constable. Why aren't you in uniform?'

'Because,' retorted Hamish sharply, 'I am very sick. Did Priscilla no' tell you?'

She shook her head. 'Come ben, then,' said Hamish sulkily. Here he was, at death's door, and Priscilla had not even bothered to tell her friend he was sick. He began to feel shaky and ill again. Priscilla had left the living-room fire set with paper and logs. He struck a match and lit it.

Jane sank down into an armchair and crossed her long legs.

'The trouble,' she said, suddenly leaning forward so that her blouse plunged alarmingly low at the front, 'is that you are not going the right way about curing your cold. It is the common cold, isn't it?'

Hamish, now in the armchair opposite, took out a handkerchief and blew his nose miserably by way of reply.

'It is all in your mind,' said Jane. 'The weather has been very cold and so you began to feel you might get one and your mind conveyed that message to the rest of your body and so you got one. Put your index fingers on either side of your head, just at the temples, and repeat after me, concentrating all the while, "I have not got a cold. I am fit and well."'

'Havers,' said Hamish crossly.

'There you have it,' said Jane triumphantly. 'You have just told me what I had already guessed.'

'That you were havering?' commented Hamish rudely.

'No, no. That you want to have a cold and make everyone feel sorry for you.' She leaned back and uncrossed and crossed her legs. Embarrassed, Hamish looked at the ceiling.

'What is the difficulty you're in?' Hamish asked the lampshade. He found those flashing legs and thighs unnerving.

'I think someone might be trying to kill me.'

Hamish's hazel eyes focused on her. 'Did you tell someone else how to get rid of their cold?'

'Do be serious. Oh, perhaps I am imagining it, but a rock did hurtle down last week close to my head, and then there was the bathroom heater. I had run my bath and was just about to step into it when the wall heater came tumbling down, right into the bath. I called in a local builder, but he said the heater had probably just come loose as the plaster was damp.'

'Did you think of telling the local policeman?'

'The local policeman is Sandy Ferguson. Have you heard of him?'

'Yes,' said Hamish, remembering the famous day in Strathbane when Sandy Ferguson, drunk as usual, had told Detective Chief Inspector Blair exactly what he thought of him and had been subsequently banished to the Hebrides. 'Never say you're living on Eileencraig!'

Jane nodded.

'You'd better begin at the beginning,' said Hamish.

Jane looked doubtfully at the thin, red-haired constable in the old dressing-gown and then made up her mind.

'I run a health farm called The Happy Wanderer . . .'

'Oh, my.' Hamish winced.

'Called The Happy Wanderer,' went on Jane firmly, 'on the island of Eileencraig. Part of the healthy regime is brisk walking. I decided to go into business for myself after my divorce two years ago. It had been pretty successful. Health farms are the coming thing. I not only teach people how to have a healthy body but how to get in touch with their innermost feelings. Do you read me?'

'Sort of.'

'Well, the islanders are a clannish lot and don't like incomers, so I thought perhaps the rock thingie and the heater thingie were, well, *pranks* to scare me away. That was until I spoke to Mrs Bannerman at Skulag, the main village, and she read my tea-leaves and she saw death in them. Someone from far away was trying to kill me, she said. That's when I began to worry about my guests.'

'Paying guests?'

'No, the health farm is closed for the winter. Friends.'

'Who are these friends?'

'People I invited to spend Christmas with me. There's a Mr and Mrs Todd from Glasgow, he's in real estate; then there's Harriet Shaw, the writer.'

'Haven't heard of her,' commented Hamish.

'*You* wouldn't. She writes cookery books. There's Sheila and Ian Carpenter from Yorkshire – dear, dear people, he's a farmer.' Jane threw back her head and gave a merry laugh. She's practised that laugh in front of the mirror, thought Hamish suddenly. 'And,' said Jane, suddenly looking solemn, 'there's my ex.'

'Your ex-husband?'

'Yes, John. He's been working so hard. He does need a holiday.'

'Who divorced whom?'

The large eyes opposite shifted away from him slightly. 'Oh, we were very civilized about it. A mutual agreement. Well, there you are. What do you think?'

'Are they still there?'

'Oh, yes. After what Mrs Bannerman saw in the tea-leaves, I felt I had to get away to meditate and heard Priscilla had fallen on hard times and so I thought I would hop over for a couple of nights just to *think*. What do *you* think?'

'First of all,' said Hamish, 'I believe Eileencraig is a weird enough place to give anyone the jitters. You're right. They hate incomers. I think the heater and the rock were plain and simple accidents. But when the villagers heard you were going to visit Mrs Bannerman to get your fortune told, they must have put her up to giving you a fright. That, in my opinion, is all there is to it.'

She leaned forward and the blouse plunged alarmingly again. 'Do you know,' said Jane in that breathy, sexy voice of hers, 'you are a *most* intelligent man.' She threw back her head and gave that practised merry laugh of hers again. 'I was so edgy that when Priscilla told me about you, I was going to invite you to come back with me for Christmas and bribe you with the promise of an old-fashioned dinner of turkey and mince pies.'

Hamish sat stricken. Then he said carefully, 'On the other hand, I cannot help thinking about my Aunt Hannah, her that lives in San Francisco.'

'Yes?'

'She always swore she would neffer set foot in Scotland again, but a wee woman in the Chinese quarter told her fortune and said she would soon be going on a long journey to her native land. She forgot all about it, until one day she found she had booked a plane flight home to Scotland. Then there wass ma cousin Jamie . . .'

Jane's mouth fell a little open as she gazed at him.

'Yes, Jamie,' said Hamish in a crooning voice. 'He was at this game fair and a gypsy woman had a caravan there. Jamie and his friends had a wee bit too much to drink and they urged Jamie to have his tea-leaves read. Into that black caravan he went, laughing something awful and telling that gypsy

225

woman it was all a load of rubbish. But she read the leaves.'

'And?' urged Jane, who was goggling at him.

'And the gypsy woman said, "Laugh ye may, but look out for your life. Next week, someone is going to try to kill you." Well, Jamie, he thought she was trying to get revenge because he had laughed at her, but the very next week –' Hamish lowered his voice to a whisper – 'he wass in Aberdeen, looking for work on the rigs and someone mugged him.'

'No!'

'Oh, yes, and stuck a knife in his side. He's lucky to be alive.'

'I have never jeered at the paranormal,' said Jane. 'You may think me foolish, Hamish, but I am begging you now to come with me. Can you get any leave?'

'I happen to be on leave as from tomorrow,' said Hamish, 'but with this cold . . .'

'I have very good central heating,' said Jane, 'and you will be looked after like a king.'

'Seeing as how you are a friend of Priscilla's, I'll force myself to go,' said Hamish.

When Priscilla arrived to pick Jane up, she looked amazed to hear that Hamish intended to travel to Eileencraig with Jane and stay there for Christmas. 'I'll talk to you later,' said Priscilla.

Jane's eyes fell on Towser. 'No dogs,' she said.

'Perhaps I can take Towser.' Priscilla looked doubtful. 'But I'll talk to you later, Hamish.'

After they had gone, Hamish poured himself a celebratory whisky. He had nearly blown it. If he had not invented those tales about his relatives and the tea-leaves, he might not have had a comfortable Christmas to look forward to.

Priscilla arrived that evening, looking cross. 'What on earth are you up to, Hamish Macbeth? Jane told me some rubbish about tea-leaves and I was leaving it to you to talk her out of it. Besides, what will your family think?'

'They don't want me,' said Hamish. 'Aunt Hannah's coming over from the States and that means I have to stay away. She cannae stand me. Och, I forgot the presents for the family. I was supposed to take them over at the end of the week.'

He looked at Priscilla pleadingly.

'All right! All right!' she said impatiently. 'I'll take Towser *and* the presents over to Rogart. In fact, I'll do it tomorrow and get it over with. There's bad weather forecast. The wind's turned to the east and all that slush is beginning to freeze like mad. I can't help feeling guilty about letting you trick Jane into that invitation, but seeing as how you've got a holiday and nowhere else to go, and seeing as how Jane is simply loaded, I suppose it should be all right.'

'You're always rushing.' Hamish tried to take her coat. 'Sit down for a bit.'

'No, no, I daren't. We've got a party of Spanish aristocrats. They speak perfect English, which is something Daddy refuses to understand, so he shouts at them and thinks if he puts *h* in front of everything, he's speaking Spanish. You should hear him roaring, 'H'everything h'OK?'

She threw her arms about him and gave him an impulsive hug. 'Be good, Hamish. Have a merry Christmas.'

'Merry Christmas,' echoed Hamish as she hurtled out of the door and banged it behind her. He could still feel the warmth of her thin body for a few moments after she had gone, and into his mind came slight, sad, bittersweet memories of the days when he had loved her so much.

The sun came up at ten in the morning to shine over a glittering icy landscape, a glaring yellow sun which forecast high gales to come. True to her promise, Priscilla collected Towser and the presents and set out on the long road to Rogart while Hamish climbed into Jane's Range Rover and headed down the coast. Jane said that a fishing boat would take them out to the island, as no passenger ferry was due there for another week. She was wearing a short leather jerkin over another short skirt and a pair of black leather thigh-boots. She discoursed at length on her innermost feelings as she drove competently down the winding twisty roads beside the glittering sea. If anyone ever issued a press handout about innermost feelings, it would read rather like Jane's conversation, reflected Hamish. She suffered, she said, from low self-esteem and a perpetual feeling of insecurity, and Hamish wondered if she really felt anything much at all. She seemed to be reciting something she had read about someone else rather than talking about herself. He wished suddenly he had not taken her up on her invitation. It would have been fun if he could have gone to his parents' instead with Priscilla. He had not seen much of Priscilla of late. She was always busy, always rushing.

Priscilla drove under the shadow of the towering Sutherland mountains. Great gusts of wind tore at the car and then the snow began to fall. She switched on her headlights and leaned forward, peering through the driving snow, watching the road in front uneasily as it became whiter and whiter. She heaved a sigh of relief when at last she saw the orange street lights of Lairg ahead. Not far to go.

The road from Lairg to Rogart is quite a good one, although it seemed, that afternoon, to be disappearing rapidly under the snow. Priscilla stopped outside Rogart and studied a map Hamish had drawn for her. The Macbeths' house was above the village, up on the hills.

She was feeling tired with the strain of driving so long in the howling blizzard. She crawled up the hill road at the back of Rogart, peering anxiously in front of her. And then, with great relief, she saw the telephone-box that Hamish had drawn at a crossroads on his map. The entrance to the croft was a few yards up on the left. The car groaned and chugged its way along. She had almost decided she would need to stop and get out and walk when she dimly saw the low shape of a white croft house. Hoping she was not driving across the front garden, she drew up outside the door and sat for a moment, rubbing her tired eyes.

The kitchen door opened and the small round figure of Hamish's mother appeared. 'It's yourself, Priscilla,' she cried in amazement. 'And the dog! Where's Hamish?'

'It's a long story,' said Priscilla, climbing out of the car and walking with Towser into the welcoming warmth of the house. There seemed to be Macbeths everywhere, both large and small, and all with Hamish's flaming-red hair.

'I'll just leave Towser and the presents from Hamish, and then I'd better get back,' said Priscilla, after explaining where Hamish was.

'Nonsense,' said Mrs Macbeth. 'Sit yourself down, lassie. You're no' going anywhere tonight.'

She was hustled into the living-room and pressed down into a battered armchair by the fire. A glass of whisky was put into her hand. Priscilla realized for the first time in months that she was tired, bone-tired. Her eyes began to droop and the empty glass was gently removed from her hand. Soon she was fast asleep.

'Did ye ever see such a mess o' skin and bone?' said Mrs Macbeth, looking down at Priscilla. 'It's fattening up that lassie needs. She cannae go anywhere until the roads are clear. And it's just as well. Hamish said that faither o' hers was a slave-driver, horrible wee man that he is. I think we'll keep her here for a bit until she gets some rest.'

Mr Macbeth smiled at her vaguely and retreated behind his newspaper. He had given up arguing with his wife exactly two weeks after they were married.

'I do rely on Priscilla for advice,' Jane was saying as she drove competently along a stone jetty. 'We'll just wait in the car until we see the boat coming, Hamish, and then I'll garage it in that lock-up over there. Yes, Priscilla. So cool. Such a relaxing girl. Oh, there's the boat.'

Hamish climbed out of the warmth of the Range Rover and shivered on the jetty. Small pellets of snow were beginning to blow through the rising wind. He looked over the sea and experienced a slight feeling of uneasiness, almost dread, and wished he had not come.